Madison
the Magic Show
Fairy

Madison
the Magic Show
Fairy

by Daisy Meadows

ORCHARD BOOKS

www.rainbowmagic.co.uk

Who likes talent shows? Not me!
So, goblins, listen carefully,
Each Showtime Fairy has a star,
Their magic glitters near and far.

Now do exactly as I say,
And steal these magical stars away,
Then, when our wicked work is done,
We can spoil all showtime fun!

Contents

All the Fun of the Fair!

Rachel Walker gazed excitedly out of the car window, as her mum parked. A short distance away she could see a helter-skelter, a spinning tea-cups ride, dodgems, and all sorts of sideshows and stalls. "This is going to be fun!" she said to her best friend, Kirsty Tate, who was sitting next to her in the back seat.

9

Kirsty grinned. "It looks great," she said, her eyes shining.

Kirsty had come to stay at Rachel's house for a whole week during the October half-term, and it was lovely to be with Rachel again. The girls always had the best time when they were together… and the most exciting fairy adventures, too! They had helped the fairies in many different ways before, although their parents and other friends had no idea about their amazing secret.

10

"There," Mrs Walker said, switching off the engine. She turned to smile at the girls. "Do you want me to come in with you?"

Rachel shook her head. "We'll be fine, Mum," she said. "We're meeting Holly near the helter-skelter in ten minutes, so we'll go straight there."

"OK," said Mrs Walker. "I'll be back here at three o'clock to pick you up. Have a good time."

"We will," Kirsty said politely. "Thanks, Mrs Walker. See you later."

11

The girls went through the park
gates. There was a sign advertising the
'Tippington Variety Show'
which was to be
held at the end
of the week,
and Rachel
pointed at
it. "Mum's
got us tickets
for that as a
treat," she said.

"A variety
show… that's one
with lots of different kinds
of acts on, isn't it?" Kirsty asked.

Rachel nodded. "Yes," she said. "And
they're holding auditions for the acts
every day this week. Today they're

auditioning for magicians. Lots of the
schools around here have put forward
performers, and the best one
will appear in the
Variety Show
next Saturday.
My friend Holly's
been picked from
our school to
audition, so I said
we'd cheer her on."
The girls walked
through the fair together.
Lots of people were enjoying
the rides, or trying their luck on the
stalls. They passed a hook-a-duck stall,
a big rollercoaster and dodgems, and
could smell sweet candyfloss, salty chips
and fried onions. The auditions were

taking place in a tent next to the
helter-skelter.

"There's Holly," Rachel said, waving
at her. "Wait till you see her magic tricks,
Kirsty, she's really good. She's been
practising non-stop lately."

Kirsty grinned. "And magic is
something we know *all* about," she said.
"I wonder if we'll meet any more fairies
this holiday?"

"I hope so," Rachel said, lowering her
voice as they approached Holly. "Oh,
Kirsty, I really hope so!"

A Disappearing Trick

"Hello," Holly said, as Rachel and Kirsty went over to her. "You must be Kirsty. I've heard so much about you!"

Kirsty smiled. "Hi, it's lovely to meet you," she said. "Are you all set for your audition?"

"I think so," Holly said. "Shall we go into the tent? I can do a last-minute practice session for you both if you like."

"Yes, please," Rachel said, as she and Kirsty followed Holly inside the tent. There was a large stage with rows of seats in front of it. Behind the stage, hidden by some curtains, were lots of other children, all practising their tricks before the auditions began. Rachel waved as she saw Holly's mum ironing the cloak that Holly was going to wear for her performance.

The three girls found a quiet corner so that Holly could rehearse in front of them.

"First, I will perform my amazing disappearing coin trick," she said in a deep, dramatic voice. "I will make a coin vanish… and then reappear somewhere very unexpected."

"This is a good one," Rachel whispered to Kirsty. She'd seen Holly do this trick lots of times before, and there had been a big cheer at school when she'd made the coin appear from behind the headteacher's ear!

Holly held up a silver coin in one hand. "Here is the coin," she declared, then passed her other hand across it. "And now the coin has… Oh. *Not* vanished," she said sounding puzzled.

Rachel bit her lip. Poor Holly must be nervous. This hadn't happened before. "Try again," she said encouragingly.

Holly held up the coin once more. "Here is the coin," she repeated, then passed her other hand over it a second time. "And now the coin has…" She stared at the silver coin, still where it had originally been. "Why isn't it vanishing?" she muttered in dismay.

"Try another trick," Rachel urged.
"How about the one where you guess
the card that someone has picked?"

Holly put down the coin, still looking
baffled. "OK," she said, taking a deck
of cards from her pocket. She spread the
cards in a fan before Kirsty. "Pick a card,
any card," she said. "Don't show me what
it is, just have
a good look and
remember it."

Kirsty slid
out a card
and held it
up so that
she and
Rachel could
see it. It was the
Four of Hearts.

Holly cut the deck of cards in two, and asked Kirsty to put her card in between them. "Now I cut the pack again," Holly said, splitting it, "and a second time, and your card should be on the top." She held the pack out towards Kirsty. "Take a look."

Kirsty picked off the top card. It was the Queen of Spades.

"Is this your card?" Holly asked.

Kirsty shook her head. "Sorry, no," she said.

Holly tried again. "Is this your card?" she asked, holding up the Seven of Clubs.

Again, Kirsty shook her head. "No," she said, feeling bad for Holly.

Holly gave a huge sigh. "I don't know what's wrong with me," she said, putting her cards back in her pocket.

22

"Maybe it's just nerves," Rachel said. "I'm sure you'll be all right once the audition starts."

But Holly didn't look so sure. "I've got a really complicated disappearing trick later in my act," she fretted. "If I can't even get these simple tricks right, I've got no hope of pulling that one off." She put her head in her hands. "It's going to be a disaster!"

Rachel and Kirsty exchanged glances. Poor Holly! "You'll be fine," Kirsty said kindly. "I bet everyone else is nervous too."

Holly nodded. "Thanks," she said. "I'd better get Abracadabra ready now. He's my rabbit, and he has a big part to play in the act."

She went to the back of the tent where she'd stored her props...then gave a gasp. The door of her rabbit's cage was wide open...and there was no sign of Abracadabra anywhere!

"Oh no!" she cried. "This is getting worse and worse. Will you help me look for him?"

"Of course," Rachel said. She opened
Holly's magic trunk, but the rabbit wasn't
in there.

Kirsty lifted up Holly's magic top hat,
but Abracadabra wasn't there either.
But then something caught her eye. As
she moved the hat, she was sure she saw
a sparkle fly out from it – and it looked
very much like a fairy sparkle!

She turned the hat over carefully and
felt around inside. Aha! The bottom of
it lifted straight out...

and inside, hiding
in a secret
compartment,
was a
pretty
little
fairy!

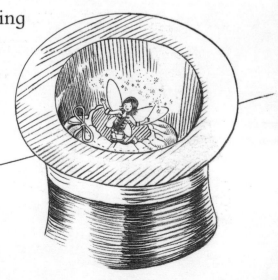

Flight to Fairyland

Kirsty's mouth fell open in astonishment, and she was just about to let out a cry of delight, when the fairy put a finger to her lips. Kirsty nodded and closed her mouth again. She knew that she and Rachel had to keep the fairies a secret – nobody else could know about them. She nudged Rachel, showing her what she'd discovered, and a smile lit up Rachel's face.

"Um… Holly, we'll look outside for Abracadabra," she called, shielding the hat with her back, so that the fairy could fly out unseen.

Holly was hunting through a pile of clothes, looking increasingly desperate. "Thank you," she called. "Oh, where could he *be*?"

Meanwhile, the fairy had fluttered out of the hat with a swirl of colourful sparkles.

Rachel held open her jacket pocket, and the fairy swooped down into it.

Then the two girls hurried out of the tent to find somewhere quiet to talk to the fairy. Both of them felt fizzy with excitement. Was this the start of another fairy adventure?

They ducked under the helter-skelter where they'd be out of sight, and the fairy flew out of Rachel's pocket and landed on her hand. She had shoulder-length dark hair, sparkly green eyes and was wearing a cute jacket and shorts with black leggings underneath.

"Hello!" the fairy said in a silvery voice that sounded as if tiny bells were ringing. "My name's Madison, and I'm one of the Showtime Fairies. You two must be Kirsty and Rachel. I'm so glad to meet you. The fairies badly need your help!"

"What's happened?" Rachel asked.

Madison gave a little sigh. "You've met Jack Frost before, haven't you?"

"Yes," Kirsty said. Jack Frost was a cold, spiky creature who was always doing mean things to the fairies. "What has he done now?"

"It's thanks to Jack Frost that your friend Holly can't perform her magic tricks properly," Madison said. "But I can explain better if you come to Fairyland with me now – is that all right?"

"Of course!" Rachel and Kirsty chorused in the same breath. They always loved going to Fairyland. It was the most wonderful place in the world! They knew that time would stand still in the human world whilst they were away.

Madison waved her magic wand. "Thank you!" she said, as rainbow sparkles streamed out of it, and whizzed around the girls. In the next moment, they felt themselves shrinking smaller and smaller, and being spun into the air, so fast that everything became a blur.

Seconds later, Rachel and Kirsty felt themselves land, and the sparkles faded away. They could see the turrets and spires of the Fairyland Palace, and lots of little toadstool houses in the distance. They were back in Fairyland, and they were fairies themselves, with their own gauzy wings on their backs!

Rachel smiled and flapped her wings. How she loved being able to fly! Then she realised she was in a part of Fairyland she'd never seen before. "Where are we?" she asked.

"This is the Fairyland Theatre," Madison explained. "We fairies are having a talent show too, like the one in your world. This is one of the rehearsals."

The girls gazed around. There was a long stage, with a semi-circle of toadstool seats in front of it. A beautiful garden surrounded the audience area, and the air was sweet with the scent of roses. On the stage itself were some fairies the girls recognised – the Music Fairies and the Dance Fairies!

Kirsty smiled to see their friends… but her smile soon disappeared. The rehearsal wasn't going well at all. Victoria the Violin Fairy's bow suddenly broke in half, and Danni the Drum Fairy's drums toppled over, tripping up Jade the Disco Fairy and sending her tumbling to the ground. "Ouch!" Jade wailed, clutching her ankle.

"Oh dear," Rachel said. "That doesn't look good."

"No, it isn't," came a new voice, and the girls turned to see six other fairies approaching. "Hi," said the pretty auburn-haired fairy who'd just spoken to them. "I'm Isla the Ice Star Fairy, and you must be Kirsty and Rachel. Thank you so much for agreeing to help us."

The other Showtime Fairies introduced themselves as Leah the Theatre Fairy, Alesha the Acrobat Fairy, Darcey the Dance Diva Fairy, Amelia the Singing Fairy and Taylor the Talent Show Fairy.

"We Showtime Fairies know that everyone has a special talent or skill," Alesha began explaining. "And we use our magic stars to ensure that everyone can use these talents and skills to their very best ability."

"We decided to organise a special
Fairyland talent show in
honour of Queen Titania
and King Oberon,"
Taylor added, "and
it was going to
be wonderful.
Everyone was so
excited – well,
apart from
horrible
Jack Frost,
of course."

"He doesn't like
anyone having fun,"
Leah put in with
a sigh. "And that's
why he decided to
spoil the show."

"Oh, no,"
Rachel said.
"Trust Jack
Frost to do
something
mean!"

"What
happened?"
Kirsty asked.

"He knew
that the power of our
magic stars would make the acts at the
Fairyland talent show extra special,"
Darcey replied. "So while we were
rehearsing our act together yesterday,
he stole the magic stars from the ends of
our wands, and told his goblin servants
to sneak into the human world and hide
them there."

"And that's why your friend's magic tricks were going wrong," Madison explained. "Because while our wands are missing their stars, everyone has lost their talents, both here in Fairyland, and in the human world."

Kirsty gasped. "That's awful," she said. "The talent show here will be a washout – and the magic show auditions will be a disaster. We've got to find those stars!"

The Great Gobbolino

"Let's go back to the auditions," Madison said. "I had a feeling my magic star was somewhere around the funfair. If we find it quickly, we might be able to make things right there, at least."

She sprinkled some fairy dust over Rachel and Kirsty, and another sparkly whirlwind whizzed around them, lifting them off the ground and spinning them away very fast. When they landed, they were girls again, and back under the helter-skelter.

"First things first, let's find Abracadabra," Madison said in a business-like way. She used some more fairy dust to magic up a fat orange carrot in Rachel's hand. "No rabbit will be able to resist that!" she said with a grin, then flew back into Rachel's pocket.  "Let's see if we can tempt Holly's rabbit out of his hiding place."

Abracadabra must have smelled the carrot and felt hungry because as soon as the girls and Madison re-entered the tent, he hopped out from under a table, his little nose twitching.

"Oh, good boy,"
Kirsty said,
hurrying to
scoop him up.

Rachel
held out the
carrot and
he nibbled
happily at
the end of
it. "Holly!
We've found
Abracadabra!" she called.

"Thank you!" Holly cried, looking
relieved as she ran over.

"Just in time, too," her mum said. "The
auditions are starting soon. You've just got
time to run through your act once more
with me." Kirsty and Rachel decided to

leave Holly in peace while she practised, and walked around the tent, watching the other children rehearsing.

"Keep your eyes peeled for anything suspicious," Madison whispered from her hiding place. "I'm getting a strong sense that my star is somewhere nearby!"

There were people practising card tricks, one boy rehearsing a rope trick, and another girl pulling a string of coloured scarves from her pocket. Then Rachel stopped walking as she saw someone wearing a green cape and top hat, surrounded by several schoolboys in bright green blazers and school caps. There was something odd about them, Rachel thought, frowning. Then she

spotted the enormous green feet poking
out from the magician's cape – just as
Kirsty noticed the long, green
noses of the schoolboys…
"Goblins!" they both
hissed at the same
time. "Oh, no."
"Oh, *yes*,
you mean,"
Madison said.
"That means
my star is
nearby. But
where, I wonder?"
They watched as
a variety show official
came over to the goblins
with a clipboard. "And who
do we have here?" he asked.

"We're from Icy Towers school," one of the smallest goblins replied. "This is the Great Gobbolino."

"The Great Gobbolino... ahh, yes," said the official, ticking off the name on his list. "Hmm," said Madison thoughtfully. "I think it's time for some real magic. Let's find somewhere quiet so that I can turn you into fairies again. Then we can keep close to the goblins without them seeing us, hopefully."

The girls slipped out of the tent and
Madison worked her magic, turning them
back into tiny fairies. They fluttered
inside again to see what the goblins were
doing – and discovered that they were
causing lots of trouble.

One goblin had knocked over
somebody's card trick, getting all the
cards in the wrong order. Another had
'accidentally' become
tangled in the string of
coloured scarves and torn
them. And Gobbolino
himself trod on
somebody's top
hat, which gave a
loud crack, as if the
secret compartment
in it had just broken!

"They're going to wreck the whole show," Rachel said despairingly. But then she noticed a shimmering light from Gobbolino's cloak pocket. Was the magic star in there? There was only one way to find out.

Daringly, she swooped through the air and hovered by the rim of Gobbolino's deep pocket. She peered inside and saw a small, glowing star, shimmering all the colours of the rainbow.

She was just about to sneak into the pocket to grab it, when she heard one of the other goblins hiss a warning. "Hey! Gobbolino! Fairy alert. Run for it!"

And then, in the very next instant, Gobbolino looked down and saw Rachel. His eyes narrowed briefly, then he flicked her away with his knobbly green fingers and dashed out of the tent with the other goblins.

Rachel flapped her wings desperately as she tumbled down through the air, and only just managed to stop herself falling to the floor. "Quick, after them!" she called to Kirsty and Madison. "We mustn't let them get away!"

Wand Worries

Rachel, Kirsty and Madison all zoomed after the running goblins who headed straight for the dodgems. The goblins hopped into a couple of empty dodgem cars and began swerving around madly at top speed. "Let's stay close to Gobbolino," Kirsty said, pointing him out. "We might be able to grab the star while he's concentrating on steering his car."

They fluttered down silently to land just inside the dodgem car, next to Gobbolino himself. His face was screwed up in determination as he drove, then he glanced over his shoulder, obviously looking for the fairies. "I think we've lost them, guys," he cackled happily. "They were too slow for us goblins!"

Kirsty and Rachel wanted to giggle at his words. Little did Gobbolino know that they were right next to him – and not 'lost' at all! Madison, meanwhile, fluttered around to Gobbolino's cloak pocket which was hanging tantalisingly open.

She grinned at Kirsty and Rachel and made a thumbs-up sign…but then another dodgem crashed into Gobbolino's car, jolting them all. Startled, Madison flew into the air… and Gobbolino saw her, and promptly grabbed hold of her!

"Aha!" he snarled. "What have we here? An interfering fairy, eh?"

"Let me go!" Madison cried, squirming in his grasp.

Kirsty and Rachel flew up into the air, too, wondering what to do. How could they help their new friend?

"I said… LET GO!" Madison shouted, wrenching herself free. But as she escaped from his big fingers, Gobbolino snatched at her wand… and it fell from Madison's hand.

"Wahey!" Gobbolino cheered, holding the wand. It

grew to human-size as he held it, and
a grin spread across his face. He reached
in his pocket for the magic star and
slotted it onto the wand. "Hey, boys!" he
yelled to the other
goblins, driving
to the edge of
the dodgem
rink and
leaping out.
He waved
the wand
in the air
above his
head. "I
know what'll
be even more
fun than ruining the
auditions. Winning them!"

57

And with that, he raced back towards the theatre, with his goblin friends hurrying after him.

Kirsty, Rachel and Madison fluttered outside the dodgem rink. Madison looked very pale and shocked. "This is *awful*," she said faintly. "It's bad enough that the goblins can get extra magic skills from having the star, but if they use the wand to make real magic on stage, they could give away the secret of Fairyland!"

"We've got to stop them," Rachel said at once. "If you turn us back into girls, we'll have more chance of getting the wand back now that it's much bigger."

Madison had just a small amount of fairy dust left, and she used some to magic the girls back to their usual size. They rushed back to the audition tent.

The audience had taken their seats by now, and the judging panel were walking on stage to cheers and applause. The auditions were about to begin!

Rachel, Kirsty and Madison rushed backstage, where the atmosphere felt tense. It seemed that nobody wanted to audition first after so many things had gone wrong in their rehearsals! But not everyone was nervous, of course.

"I'll go first," said Gobbolino, pushing his way to the front of the queue, and clambering onto the stage.

"How can we stop him?" Madison wondered despairingly, as his goblin friends called out suggestions for what Gobbolino should do.

"Turn the judges green!" one shouted.

"Turn the audience into frogs!" called another.

"I know," Kirsty said, thinking quickly. "Rachel and I will go on as his assistants. Can you magic us some outfits, Madison?"

Madison sprinkled her last pinch of fairy dust over the girls, and glittery dresses appeared on them, instead of their ordinary clothes. Then they hurriedly borrowed Holly's hat with Abracadabra inside, as well as a long string of coloured scarves.

"Ready?" Kirsty said, feeling her heart pound with nerves. "Let's do it."

And she and Rachel walked on stage, with Madison hiding behind Kirsty's ponytail. All of them felt on edge. They had to get this right – or it would end in total disaster!

Star of the Show

The audience clapped politely at the new arrivals. Gobbolino, meanwhile, looked surprised. "Good afternoon," Rachel said, bowing. "We are the Famous Faireenies. And we challenge the Great Gobbolino to a magic duel!"

The audience clapped again, obviously thinking this was part of the act. "We don't need a *wand* to perform magic tricks," Kirsty said, looking scornfully at Madison's wand which was still in Gobbolino's hand. "We use the power of magic words. Like this!"

She gestured to Rachel who was holding the top hat. Rachel chanted some made-up magical-sounding words, then pulled out Abracadabra with a flourish.

The audience cheered, and Gobbolino
gaped. "How did you do *that*?" he
marvelled.

"That's nothing," Kirsty said airily. "For
our next trick, we will tie up the Great
Gobbolino without even touching
him." She rattled off a string
of magical-sounding
words and held
up one end of
the coloured
scarves. This
was Madison's
cue to
fly out
from her
hiding
place and
grab hold of it.

Then, making sure she was hidden
behind the scarf, Madison flew with it
round and round Gobbolino until he
was completely tied up. The audience,
of course, couldn't see Madison, and
thought the scarves were
moving on their own.
"Amazing!"
they cheered,
clapping louder
than ever.
"Bravo!"
Soon
Gobbolino
was tightly
tied up, with
his arms pinned
to his sides by
the magic scarves.

"Let me go!" he wailed, and the audience laughed, still thinking this was part of the act.

"We'll let you go… if you hand over the wand," Rachel told him.

The audience began chanting, "Hand it over! Hand it over!" and Gobbolino,

knowing he was beaten, opened his hand so that Kirsty could take the wand from him.

The audience cheered and stamped their feet as Madison flew back around Gobbolino, untying him, and setting him free.

Then Gobbolino slunk from the stage,
and the girls bowed, to great applause.

"Wonderful," one of the judges said.

"A fantastic start to the show," another
smiled. "Thank you, girls!"

Madison hid herself in Kirsty's ponytail again, and the girls went off stage. They gave the hat and Abracadabra back to Holly, and the coloured scarves back to their owner, then found a quiet corner so that Madison could magic her star-tipped wand back to its Fairyland size. Then she used it to change the girls back into their ordinary clothes once more.

"Thank you *so* much for helping me," she said happily, spinning around in mid-air, with a swirl of glittering sparkles. "Now I can make the rest of the magic show auditions go really well... thanks to you two!"

"It was fun," Kirsty said, smiling.

"I'm glad we could help," Rachel agreed.

They said goodbye to Madison, then went to find seats in the audience, just in time to see Holly step on stage to begin her act. It went brilliantly! All her tricks went perfectly, especially the last one, where she made the audience believe that a volunteer from the audience had disappeared inside her magic trunk, and then made them reappear again. She received a round of thunderous applause at the end, and left the stage beaming.

At the end of the auditions, the judges announced their favourite contestant. "Our winning act, who will take part in the Tippington Variety Show at the end of the week, is... HOLLY HAMILTON!"

A huge cheer went up as Holly came back on stage, her cheeks pink with delight. Kirsty and Rachel clapped until their hands felt numb, smiling at each other happily. "One thing's for sure," Rachel said to Kirsty, over the sound of the crowd, "we'll be seeing a *lot* more magic this holiday!"

Now it's time for Kirsty and
Rachel to help...

Leah the Theatre Fairy

Here's an exclusive extract...

A Grand
Old Theatre

"Oh, this is amazing!" Kirsty exclaimed.
She stared out of the car window at
the grand old theatre with its carved
mahogany doors, mirrored glass and
ornate, old-fashioned lamps hanging
outside. There was a painted sign over
the entrance with *The Swan Theatre*
written in golden letters. "I can't wait
to see inside."

"It's really beautiful, Kirsty," Rachel
said as her mum stopped the car. "The
theatre's Victorian, and it still looks just

like it did in the olden days!"

"I saw the pantomime *Aladdin* here last Christmas," Zac added. He was one of Rachel's school friends. "It was brilliant."

"Thank you for the lift, Mrs Walker," said Tanya, another of Rachel's friends.

"I hope the rehearsal goes well," Mrs Walker said, "And I'll pick you all up in a couple of hours."

Rachel, Kirsty, Zac and Tanya jumped out of the car. The Swan Theatre was just outside Tippington town, and it was too far for them to walk there. That was probably why she'd never seen the theatre when she'd stayed with Rachel before, Kirsty thought.

"Thank you for inviting me for half-term, Rachel," Kirsty said as they went up the marble steps to the entrance doors...

RAINBOW magic®

Make friends with the fairies
on our exciting new website,
and enjoy games, sneak peeks
and lots more!

www.rainbowmagicbooks.co.uk

Sign up to the newsletter at
www.rainbowmagicbooks.co.uk
to receive exclusive extra content and the opportunity
to enter special members-only competitions. We'll send
you up-to-date info on all the Rainbow Magic books,
including the next exciting series which features
seven brand-new fairy friends!

Competition!

If you study these four pictures of Leah the Theatre Fairy very carefully you'll see that one of them is slightly different from the others. Can you work out which one is the odd one out? Make a note of the name of this book and the letter and when you have enjoyed all seven books in the Showtime Fairies series, send the answers in to us!

Mr Warwick,' she advised him. 'And your women.'

'I hardly think you're in any position to offer advice on the good character of women,' he said pointedly.

'And you are?' she demanded.

'Oh, yes, Kate. I know exactly what makes a woman run. Money, power, ambition. They will do anything for it.' And this time his smile almost reached his eyes. 'They frequently do.'

She refused to let this go unchallenged. 'Haven't you forgotten the most important emotion?'

He folded his arms and regarded her with interest. 'And what is that?'

'Love, Mr Warwick.'

'Love?' He raised one dark expressive brow in a slightly puzzled expression. 'Do you mean sex — Kate?' Her cheeks fired under his raking gaze as he stretched out a long, well-shaped hand to lift the little brooch, read her name. She jumped as his fingers brushed lightly against her breast and, beneath her white wrapover overall, her nipple

7

hardened with such shocking immediacy that he could not fail to notice. His eyes flickered to hers. 'I hadn't forgotten. But that's not an emotion. It's a weapon.'

'What did you come to the kitchen for, Mr Warwick?' she asked, turning abruptly away. Until that moment, despite his almost unbelievable rudeness, she had felt in control of the situation. Had felt able to match anything he could throw at her. But she had been fooling herself. Her heart had been locked away for so long that she had failed to appreciate the dangerous spike of sexual awareness that had mingled with the buzz of anger.

'Ice,' he said simply, in reply to her question.

'Ice?'

'Ice. You know. Little cubes of frozen water. If it's no trouble? But if you want to rush off and keep your appointment with Harry, just point me in the right direction and I'll help myself.'

She wrenched open the freezer door

and tried to remember that this man was a guest in her client's house. 'It's no trouble,' she said through gritted teeth as she grabbed a bag of ice and dumped it on the table, jabbing a hole in it, wishing it were him. She tipped some into a bowl, holding it out at the full stretch of her arm, unwilling to move any nearer, to risk further contact.

He made no move to take it. Instead he continued to regard her with a level, penetrating, oddly seductive stare that, despite her anger, or perhaps because of the flood of adrenalin rushing giddily through her veins, did something rather odd to her insides, flipping them over in a way that made her breath catch raggedly in her throat and her breast rise and fall rather too quickly.

Gripping the bowl more tightly in a desperate attempt not to betray the urgent increase in her pulse-rate, she lowered her eyes to the broad white expanse of his shirt-front, the top button unfastened to reveal his tanned throat, the silk tie long since pulled from its bow to hang loose about his neck. But he hooked his fingers under her chin, lifting her face until she could not avoid looking up at him. Five feet and four inches in her stockinged feet, she had a long way to look.

'Is there something else you want, Mr Warwick?' Her voice stuck somewhere in her throat and emerged as little more than a whisper.

For a long moment his dark eyes held her captive to a searching scrutiny, her apparently boneless legs his unwilling accomplices to this hijack. 'Perhaps I've changed my mind about dessert,' he said, at last.

Kate had thought she was angry, but now she was glad of the fury that lashed through her, restoring some semblance of sanity to her overheated body. Jason Warwick might be considered desirable by some women, but as far as she was concerned he was an arrogant, self-opinionated . . . She stopped. Forced a smile to her lips. Pride demanded a cool response.

'What exactly did you have in mind, Mr Warwick?' she asked. 'A quick fumble, like your friend Harry?' If she had thought she could shame him, she realised at once that she had made a mistake. Nothing about him changed, but his eyes sparked ominously as they scanned her face.

'In all my life . . . Kate . . . ' he paused briefly to linger on her name, investing it with the power to insult ' . . . I have never done anything even remotely the same as Harry Roberts.' His voice was as smooth and cutting as glass. 'I certainly wouldn't be cheating on my wife with the hired help in someone else's kitchen.' She took a swift step backwards, away from the drugging touch of his fingers and for a moment she thought she had escaped him. But the table dug into her back and before she could turn away he had placed his hands, either side of her, making her his prisoner. 'But then, I'm not married.'

'So it's all right?' She was at his

mercy. They both knew it, but she had had enough of lecherous men for one night. 'I'm sorry, Mr Warwick, but I'm afraid you're really not my type,' she said, holding herself rigid, eschewing an unseemly struggle in an effort to retain some semblance of poise.

'No?' He raised one eloquent brow and shrugged slightly. Then, taking the bowl of ice from her hands and putting it on the table behind her, he said, 'Shall we see?' For him this was just a game, one in which his partners were always more than willing. So he waited, making no move to meet her halfway, apparently expecting her to stand on her toes and reach up to kiss him. Kate was damned if she would.

Yet she knew that kissing Jason Warwick would be a world away from being manhandled by his fellow dinner guest. Her racing pulse, the way her body quickened mindlessly to the warm masculine scent of him, the gentle pressure of his arms as they held her captive told her so, ringing alarm bells in her head. She had thought she was immune to such careless flirtation. Heartbreak was a painful vaccination, but it had served her well over three hard years.

But this man emanated a quite irresistible magnetism and, while her head was behaving rationally, she was only too conscious that her body was not. Her lips were hot and swollen as she imagined his beautiful, passionate mouth plundering them, and there was a trembling about her midriff at the thought of his hands about her waist, drawing her close . . .

She shivered convulsively. What on earth was happening to her? Sensible, down-to-earth, cold-as-ice Kate, who never let even the most devoted of her admirers within an arm's length.

Agitated, stalling for time, she reached up to tuck a glossy black strand of hair behind her ear. Her lips parted nervously and she ran a cooling tongue across their surface. For a moment their eyes met and with a jolt like an electric shock she realised that he was angry. With her? For her apparently casual flirtation with Harry Roberts? That was surely ridiculous. Or was it with himself for so eagerly following suit?

Well, she thought, furious at his arrogant assumption that she was prepared to inflate his oversized ego a little further, he needn't get himself into a bother about it. Her grey eyes turned steely and her naturally warm voice dropped several degrees below zero. 'I'm afraid you'll just have to take my word for it that I have absolutely no desire to kiss you, Mr Warwick.'

For a moment he remained perfectly still, the slightest frown creasing his brow. Then with one swift movement his hand slid down her back and he held her against the long, hard length of his body, moulding her breasts, her hips to him, and her body quivered with a surge of longing for something she knew he could give her and in that moment she wanted more than anything in the world.

14

'Liar,' he grated out harshly. Before she could utter a protest, his mouth had staked its claim and it was too late. But in those long, blissful moments she didn't care. As desire sparked through her like a lightning strike she knew, without the slightest shadow of doubt, that he was the most desirable man she had ever met.

Her response had nothing to do with thought, or common sense. Her lips parted to his coaxing as unthinkingly as she breathed. Her breasts, hard against the broad expanse of his dress shirt, tingled deliciously as heat flickered through her veins and she let herself drown in the sensual pleasure of his tongue, sweet on hers. The kiss seemed to go on forever, her breath rising in tempo to match his, her arms long since having found their way around his neck to draw him down to her.

When finally he held her away from him Kate stared up at him, dazed, every inch of her pulsing with the sort of arousal that until that moment she

would have dismissed as the feverish
and overworked imagination of the ado-
lescent mind, and a stifled sound came
from somewhere deep in her throat.

'Your word, like any other woman's,
Kate, is worthless.' The sharp edge
to his voice jolted her roughly back to
the reality of the kitchen, the edge
of the table at her back, the humiliation
of having been kissed by a total stranger
as if one of them was going to war. And
the certain knowledge that it had been
a demonstration. Nothing more. The
blanked-out expression in his eyes
could mean nothing else. And how
could she protest? She had told him she
didn't want to kiss him and he had
called her a liar. Her lips had betrayed
her and proved him right.

'I said I didn't want to kiss you, Mr
Warwick,' she said, her voice hoarse from
a throat aching with misery. 'And that
was the truth. I didn't say I wouldn't
enjoy it.' That was what made it so
awful. At least Harry's fumbling attempt
at a pass, horrible though it had been,

had had a kind of honesty about it.

Jason Warwick had simply set out to prove a point. Whether he had gained any pleasure from kissing her it was impossible to say. His brown eyes had a natural warmth that disguised the apparent coldness of his soul. Only a vein, beating furiously at his temple, suggested any feeling, any emotion.

For a moment he stared at her, then with a fierce oath he turned away and strode from the kitchen.

'Mr Warwick,' she called, a little unsteadily, as he reached the doorway. He paused, but didn't turn. 'You've forgotten your ice.'

★   ★   ★

The telephone rang and Kate, deep in concentration adding a row of figures, jumped, lost her place, sighed and lifted the receiver. 'Kate Thornley,' she said.

'Good morning, Miss Thornley.' Kate returned the greeting, instantly recognising the silvery tones of Lady Maynard, one of her favourite clients, despite the fact that it was Tisha Maynard's kitchen that had been the scene of the appalling encounter with Jason Warwick.

'Miss Thornley, I wonder if you would be kind enough to spare me an hour today?'

'Of course. What kind of party are you planning?'

'Not a party. I'd rather not discuss it on the telephone.'

Kate stared at the telephone. That sounded ominous. Surely the man hadn't said anything about finding her in Harry Roberts' arms? Jason Warwick hadn't exactly covered himself with glory. 'I'm free at eleven-thirty. Would that be convenient?'

'I'll expect you then.'

Kate replaced the receiver and went into her bedroom to change into something more suitable than jeans for the forthcoming interview. She opened her wardrobe door and stared at her reflection in the mirror.

She had the clear, almost translucent

skin that often went with black hair. Only her cheeks were blushed delicately with pink, throwing her full mouth into vivid relief. For days after Jason Warwick had kissed her it had seemed swollen, heated, and she had been unable to bear to look at herself in a mirror. She laid a light finger on her lower lip and the pressure instantly brought his powerful image into sharp focus, and with it the memory of an urgent desire he had jolted free from its cage of ice.

'Damn him!' she swore, and reached for her one serious business suit.

★ ★ ★

It was precisely eleven-thirty when she rang the front doorbell of Lady Maynard's Belgravia house, and she was immediately shown into the drawing-room.

'How good of you to come at such short notice, Miss Thornley.' Lady Maynard, a tall, graceful figure, her fair

19

hair somewhat faded, but her dark eyes still remarkably bright, extended a beringed had. 'Please sit down.' Kate perched sedately on the edge of an exquisite sofa and waited. 'I'll come straight to the point. I have a business proposition to put to you, Miss Thornley.'

'A business proposition?' she repeated faintly. Until that moment she had not realised how tense she had become, convinced that she would have to defend herself in the face of unjust criticism. In freelance catering, where she was invited into homes and offices, reputation was everything. 'What kind of business proposition?'

'I would like to engage your professional services exclusively, that is full-time, for the next six months.' The woman raised a hand to stall Kate's expected protest. 'I have no doubt that your business in London is booming. You are a wonderful cook, and, more to the point, a splendid organiser. I can assure you that I have employed enough people who called themselves caterers to appreciate that.' She paused. 'Shall I go on? Please tell me if you are booked up so far ahead that I'm wasting my breath.'

Kate, only too aware of the sharp reminder on her desk from the bank manager about the state of her overdraft and the way bookings had fallen in the past few months, particularly for lucrative business lunches as people tightened their belts, barely hesitated. 'Please go on.'

'Have you ever been to Norfolk, Miss Thornley?'

'Norfolk?' She shook her head. 'I'm afraid not.'

'People say it's flat and maybe it is, but the light is wonderful and it has enormous skies. I live between Norwich and the coast with my nephew. At Fullerton Hall.' Her eyes were as sharp as needles. 'Maybe you have heard of it?'

Kate shook her head. 'No.'

Lady Maynard was not offended, but

nodded as if rather pleased. 'Well, it's not so grand as Blickling, although it's just as old.' She took a booklet from the table beside her, a visitor's guide, and handed it to Kate. 'It's being opened to the public very shortly.'

Kate looked at the photograph on the front cover. It was very beautiful and, despite Lady Maynard's remark, grand enough, with twin towers at each end of the façade and enormous brick chimneys, similar to those she had seen on a visit to Hampton Court. 'It's lovely.' She looked up, somewhat at a loss, and said the first thing that came into her head. 'Heating must be a bit of a problem.'

'Yes, my dear, it is.' Lady Maynard laughed. 'I knew you would be just right for the job. You're not the sort of girl to get carried away by the romance of working in an Elizabethan manor. You see the problems. That's good.'

'I'm sorry . . . ?'

'We have a sort of tearoom in the old coach house, which was perfectly adequate when we just opened the gardens once a month during the summer. But I've decided to use the Edwardian conservatory to provide somewhere rather more comfortable and offer a really special afternoon tea to tempt new visitors. Now, would you consider taking on the task of organising it, running it for the first season and training a local girl to take over from you?'

★ ★ ★

Under normal circumstances she would simply have turned it down, eager to concentrate on her own business. But these weren't normal times. Sitting at her desk, going through the figures, Kate faced the hard truth that the six-month contract she had been offered would answer all her immediate worries.

Particularly the problem of her sister's school fees. She had been banking on a scholarship for this year,

23

but it hadn't happened.

Kate felt again the sharp tug of compassion as Sam had thrown her arms about her and cried. 'I did try, Kate. Really I did.'

'I know, my love. It's not a reflection on your dancing. They just feel . . . ' She didn't continue. She didn't need to. Samantha was only fourteen, but she had come to terms with what being deaf meant. And deep down she had to sympathise with the dance academy's reaction. They had given her a place when others wouldn't even audition her and they were delighted with her progress. But there were so many deserving, talented girls . . .

It had all been there, tactfully concealed between the lines of the letter informing her that there could be no help with fees this year. With impaired hearing it would be that much harder for Sam. Beautiful, graceful, talented though she was, it was always going to be so much harder for her.

'Will I have to leave?' Sam's voice

24

had quivered slightly. Kate knew if her answer had been yes, her young sister would have taken it bravely. But she had already had to take so much in her short life and she deserved her chance. More than deserved it.

Instead Kate had held her by the shoulders, looked her straight in the face and made her a promise. 'You won't have to leave, my love. It would have been great to have had some of your fees paid, but we'll manage.' How, she didn't know. But manage they would, even if she had to take in washing. Her sister's brilliant smile was reward enough.

She glanced around her now. She hadn't told her sister about the offer she had received for the flat from her neighbour whose sister wanted to live close by. Until now there had been no point. And it would be a wrench to part with the home they had shared for three years. But with Sam away at dance school for more than half the year, it was ridiculous to keep it. They could manage with something much smaller.

And if she took the job at Fullerton Hall, she would have no expenses for at least six months. Breathing space. The first in a long time. And time to decide on the way forward. She wouldn't be losing touch entirely. She would still have her column in the *London Evening Mail*. Maybe she would even have a little time to think about the cookery book she had been collecting ideas for ever since she could remember. She picked up the telephone. There was no point in keeping Lady Maynard waiting for her answer. She would go to Norfolk as soon as Sam's Easter holidays were over.

★   ★   ★

It was their last night in the flat. Sam was already packed for school and, apart from essentials that she couldn't manage without, her own belongings were boxed up to be stored with their furniture.

Kate had cooked a special dinner and now they were draped lazily over the sofa, while Sam zapped through the television channels looking for something interesting. She paused on a chat-show and for a moment there was a close-up of the host, laughing at something his guest had said. Then the camera panned and suddenly his face was there, in front of her. Jason Warwick. And every nerve-ending jerked to attention.

It was two weeks since the dinner party but almost instinctively her hand flew to her lips. Then he smiled, not as he had smiled at her, but with warmth and humour, and she gave a soft groan of anguish.

The man had held her for a few brief moments, but in that time he seemed to have imprinted himself somehow on to the surface of her skin. Even remote, untouchable like this, her body vibrated to him, and if she put out a hand she must surely be able to push back the thick dark lock of hair that had fallen over his forehead . . .

Sam said something, but she barely heard; her eyes were fixed upon the screen, wondering that so brief an encounter could unleash such powerful emotions. Emotions she had locked firmly away when she had taken on the responsibility of providing for her sister. When David had issued his ultimatum and it seemed that her life had come to an end.

He hadn't been like Jason Warwick. David was fair, blue-eyed with an almost irresistible charm. Almost. But when it hadn't worked, that last evening they spent together, when teasing and tender kisses wouldn't move her, she had seen a different side of him. The cold, hard practical man. And she had learned her lesson well. All her love was reserved for Sam these days. They had each other, and while her sister needed her that would be enough.

And practical David had turned his blue eyes and his charm in another direction and was married within the year to a girl with parents who could

provide financial support for his business, and no burdensome younger sister whose passion for dancing drained away every spare penny. A younger sister who could dance like an angel but whose hearing had been gradually deteriorating since the car accident that had killed their parents.

That had been three years ago, and no one had been able to reach her since. Until a bored, cynical man, with the reputation for breaking the heart of any girl foolish enough to let him, had decided to teach her a lesson and kissed her until, like some latter-day fairy-tale prince, he had brought every frozen emotion painfully back to life. She shivered a little. She had never liked fairy-tales.

Kate's grey eyes narrowed as she regarded her tormentor. 'Do you think he practises his smile in front of a mirror?' she wondered out loud, her mockery a desperate attempt to destroy his power to disturb her. 'You know, Sam, like a dancer limbering up at the bar? Twenty smiles suitable for old ladies.' She tried on a patronising smile to amuse her sister. 'Twenty serious expressions enlivened by a twitch of the mouth, like so. Twenty . . . ' She blinked angry with herself for allowing him to get under her skin, but not quite able to resist watching him. Then she coloured self-consciously at her sister's knowing smirk.

The chat-show host smiled slyly at his guest. 'Come on now, Jay,' he urged with his deceptively mild Irish lilt. 'Own up. You don't really expect to find a woman these days who's prepared to conform to your oft-vaunted ideals?'

The camera closed in on him. How it loved the moulded bones of his face, she thought, as he raked long fingers through that unruly lock of hair. He regarded his inquisitor intently.

'I have never made a secret,' he said, with perfect seriousness, 'of my belief that women have two functions in life. One is in the kitchen. The other in bed.' The camera switched to the audience as it roared its approval, the men in agreement, the women apparently in hope. He acknowledged them with a slight bow. 'As you see, they don't object to either occupation.'

'Oh, God,' Kate said faintly. She felt suddenly quite sick.

'Which do you consider the most important, Jay?' his host prompted with devilish glee.

Jason Warwick's face split to reveal a row of strong, white teeth. 'I find the two combine quite naturally.' He looked straight into the camera and Kate felt his eyes were focussed only on her and she moaned softly. 'There seems to be an affinity between food and sex . . . '

There was a sudden stillness in the studio. The Irishman cleared his throat. 'Are you telling us that you've found a woman who can cook?' Getting no immediate answer, he added wickedly, 'As well?' He glanced at the audience, milking the laughter. 'It must be serious, then?'

A flash of irritation crossed Jason

31

Warwick's face, but he quickly recovered himself, lounging back in his chair, a quixotic smile firmly in place. 'Serious? My dear fellow, when have I ever been serious about anything?'

The other man laughed. 'Not about women, that's for sure. Are you going to tell us who she is?' Kate, white-faced, held her breath.

'No.' In close-up she could see the fine line etched into his cheek that might have creased when he smiled. He wasn't smiling now. 'She knows who she is. Don't you, Kate?'

Kate made a small sound in the back of her throat and Sam screamed with laughter. 'Kate Thornley, I do believe you've been keeping secrets. Did the gorgeous Jason Warwick creep up behind you when you were up to your elbows in the dishwater? Is that why you can't take your eyes off him?'

Aware that her face had gone a sickly, betraying white, she rubbed her cheeks. The teasing remark had been just a little too close to the truth for comfort.

'I don't wash up, Sam. People who can afford to hire me have machines to wash the dishes.' She forced a smile. 'Isn't it time you were in bed? It'll be a long day tomorrow.'

Sam disappeared into the kitchen for some milk and Kate turned once more to stare at the screen. Why had he done that? Used her name? It left her feeling exposed. She stood up and snapped the off button. She would be glad to get away to Norfolk. Flat and peaceful, and two hundred miles away from Jason Warwick.

2

The soft burble of the alarm woke her instantly and Kate lay quite still, for a moment uncertain where she was. Then, remembering, she flung back the cover and leapt from her bed. The room was as pretty in the early sunlight as it had been welcoming in lamplight, with its delicate cream and pink wallpaper and ivory lace floor-length curtains.

She pushed them back now and stared once more across the park to the serene vista of a lake and beyond it, on a slight rise, a small Grecian temple. Fullerton Hall was all so much larger than she had imagined, so much grander, and yet not the least bit daunting.

Her first impression had been of warm brick, flowers and, despite the carved stone beasts that defended the foot-bridge to the entrance, of welcome as the house had smiled at her, rose-pink in the dying sunshine of a fine April evening. It had quite taken her breath away.

She flexed her toes against the thick carpet, stretched and luxuriated in the simple pleasure of a hot shower without for once having to worry about the electricity bill. Then, dressed in jeans, a soft cream shirt and a fine rose sweater that reflected a blush on to her pale translucent skin, she found her way down the back stairs to the kitchen. It was warm and comfortable but Kate didn't linger, eager instead to explore the gardens nearest to the house before beginning work.

The kitchen door led to a small courtyard paved with bricks and brightened by tubs of early tulips. A hand pump next to a covered square brick wellhead had been recently painted black, as had the wrought-iron gate let into the old brick wall almost hidden by an ancient wistaria vine.

Kate opened the gate and stepped

down into the walled kitchen garden. Neat, well-raked gravel paths edged with low-growing herbs divided beds planted with early vegetable crops and tender salad plants being coaxed under cloches.

She bent to crush a few leaves of lemon thyme between her fingers, breathing in the scent. 'This,' she told a watchful robin, 'is going to be this cook's paradise.'

'Then perhaps you'd better be a little careful what you pick if you venture into the orchard.'

Kate spun around, shock sending her pulse-rate into overdrive. Jason Warwick was standing in the gateway in the wall, and regarding her inscrutably down his long, not quite straight nose. For one brief moment she dwelt on the agreeable picture of an angry fist breaking it.

'My name is not Eve, as you already know, and it's the wrong time of year for apples,' she declared vigorously as she rose, trying to ignore the athletic grace of his figure and the way his well-cut beige cord trousers clung to his hips. She concentrated on the safer area of his chest concealed under a soft wool shirt of a deeper shade. Then she averted her eyes. There was nothing safe about Jason Warwick, and it would be a grave mistake to think he was less deadly in casual clothes than in the black broadcloth and starched linen he had been wearing on their previous encounter.

'Your name is of considerably less interest at this moment than why you're trespassing in my garden,' he replied evenly, but she was not deceived. He was angry.

But he had met his match. 'Your garden indeed! I'm not the one trespassing. You are. This house belongs to Lady Maynard.'

'Does it, now?' The touch of amusement that twisted his lips made her vaguely uneasy but, hands on hips, she stood her ground as he towered over her. 'You're nearly right. But since

Tisha Maynard is my aunt and this is my home, I'm afraid you'll have to do better than that.'

'You are Tisha's nephew?'

His eyes narrowed at her use of his aunt's given name. 'I don't know what tale you've told my aunt to inveigle your way in here. Whatever it is, you'd better make your excuses and leave.' He took a step forward and grasped her firmly by the arm. 'Right now.' He turned and began to walk back to the kitchen, his fingers digging into her flesh as she resisted.

She ignored the pressure of his fingers on her arm, only fleetingly wondering why it was possible to dislike a man and everything he stood for yet still be aroused by him. 'I don't believe you,' she said. But even as the words left her lips she knew it was too horribly possible that Jason Warwick was the nephew Lady Maynard had so casually mentioned, although she couldn't understand how anyone could be casual about owning such an obnoxious relative. Perhaps that was the reason she hadn't bothered to mention who he was.

His face darkened as she dug her heels in. 'Don't make it worse by pretending not to know. What on earth do you think you're doing here?'

'Perhaps you should ask your aunt, Mr Warwick, before you start flinging accusations about.' She pulled her arm free and tugged at her sweater, then wished she hadn't as his eyes lingered on the outline of her breasts.

'Oh, I've a fair idea what you want. But if you think because I kissed you once, you'll be a welcome addition to my household, you are mistaken. This is my family home. I share it with my aunt. When I'm here, Kate, I sleep alone.'

'You must be glad of the rest,' she snapped back. 'I certainly won't be disturbing you. I had no idea you would be here.'

He gave a short, unpleasant laugh. She knew he was tall. In the close confinement of Tisha Maynard's kitchen, his height had commanded attention. But here, in the early-morning garden, there was something so physical about him that she instinctively stepped backwards. His hand shot out and caught her wrist, preventing her further retreat. 'You expect me to believe that?' His fingers tightened and he shook her slightly, like a naughty puppy. She couldn't believe the gall of the man.

'Is it so impossible?' she demanded. 'Or is your ego so inflated that you believe every woman you kiss can't wait to leap into bed with you? Let me tell you,' she continued, with reckless abandon and an equal disregard for the truth, 'I've been kissed by men just as accomplished as you!' His eyes gleamed and she fervently wished she had chosen her words more carefully. Her intended put-down had somehow developed into a compliment of sorts.

'Have you, now? Well, I suggest you pick one of them out of a hat and go right back to the lucky winner. You're not wanted here.'

'Is that so? Perhaps you should check with Lady Maynard first. Maybe she has other ideas.'

His eyes narrowed. 'Perhaps you'd better tell me.' It was not an invitation she felt capable of refusing.

'Lady Maynard has just signed a six-month contract with me. And she was the one who insisted that there should be a no-break clause. She didn't want me to change my mind.' She paused briefly. 'I can't *imagine* why she thought I might.'

He ignored the gibe. 'Six months?' He frowned. 'What on earth . . . ?' He made a dismissive gesture. 'It doesn't matter. You'll just have to come up with some particularly heart-rending reason for leaving. She won't stop you even if you signed a hundred no-break clauses. I promise,' he added fervently.

'Why should I do that, Mr Warwick? I'm extremely happy with the arrangement.' That was true as far as it went. But Tisha Maynard, in her throwaway comment about a nephew, had not thought fit to mention who he was, or she would never have come within a hundred miles of Fullerton Hall.

'That could change. Very quickly.' His eyes blackened as they insolently travelled the length of her, from narrow feet encased in immaculate white trainers, by way of slender legs and a tiny waist — a figure that, dressed in jeans, might be described as boyish by the careless onlooker — to a face that certainly could not. A full, sensuous lower lip, a nose as straight as an arrow and fine grey eyes that were flashing angry warning signals that any man would ignore at his peril. But Jason Warwick wasn't any man. He eventually arrived at the smooth coil of shining black hair that crowned her finely shaped head.

It was a look calculated to insult, to put a rocket under the blood-pressure of any woman with half an ounce of spirit, and he raised a pair of well-marked brows, inviting her response, clearly expecting an explosion that

would wreck any chance of her staying. No contract was that watertight.

But he had no idea how much she needed this job. That despite her one slip from reality in his arms, she had three years of hard-won self-control to call upon.

Kate Thornley refused Jay Warwick's invitation to self-destruct and retaliated in kind, forcing herself to return the slow, assessing examination that he had subjected her to and making very sure he understood exactly what she was doing.

She lacked his experience in these matters and therefore followed his example by beginning with his feet. They were large. Beautifully shod in hand-tooled leather, but at least a size eleven. His legs were long, and from the way the material stretched across his thighs, powerful. His hips and waist were temptingly lean and for a moment her gaze lingered, before almost reluctantly she allowed her gaze to continue over the widening chest to square,

broad shoulders.

Her impulsive challenge faltered as she reached the hard, uncompromising line of his jaw and his mouth twisted into a knowing smile. As she met his eyes, her mouth dried.

'Jay? I thought I heard your car.' The tap of an ebony cane across the brick courtyard and the swift scuff of paws announcing the arrival of Tisha Maynard and her rather scruffy little terrier smashed the threads of tension that had momentarily bound them like a web of finely spun glass. 'I didn't expect you until later, darling.' She offered her cheek to be kissed. 'I'm so glad you've introduced yourself to Miss Thornley.' She turned to her. 'Did you sleep well, Kate?'

'Yes, thank you, Tisha,' she said, conscious of Jay Warwick's eyes burning into her. 'My room is very comfortable.'

'Well, if there's anything you want, just ask.' She turned back to her nephew. 'I've managed to persuade Kate to come and run the new tearoom

for us. She's a wonderful cook and an excellent organiser. She cooked the last time you dined with me.'

'I know. We — ' his gaze flickered over Kate ' — bumped into one another. What new tearoom?'

'In the conservatory. I would have told you before, but you've been so busy with your bid for the new radio station. Besides, you said not to bother you with the details.'

'Miss Thornley is rather more than a detail. Surely you have more than enough staff?'

'No one with Kate's talent for organisation.'

'I'm sure she has many talents,' he said ambiguously. 'What exactly is she going to organise here?'

His aunt, apparently unaware that his conversation was being conducted on two levels, explained what Kate would be doing. 'So you see, Jay, you needn't worry about a thing.'

'Of course not. Who drew up the contract?' he asked, casually. 'These things need to be done properly.'

'My solicitor handled it quite as easily as yours could have done. Just because I'm old, it doesn't mean I'm foolish, Jay.'

His face softened slightly. 'I never said you were foolish, Tisha . . . ' He did not go on, apparently unwilling to destroy her pleasure in her plans, but his aunt sensed his hesitation.

'But?' she demanded, a little testily. 'I suppose you think you could have done it all a great deal better?' Kate held her breath as for a heartbeat he seemed to weigh his own feelings against hurting his aunt.

'Of course not.' He avoided Kate's eye. 'You're a clever woman and it's a lovely idea.'

Mollified, Tisha Maynard smiled at them both. 'Why don't you take Kate for a walk around the garden before breakfast, Jay? She's full of plans.'

'Is she?' He glanced at her then. 'Then a walk it will be. Come along . . . Kate. I can't wait to hear just what you have in mind.' He held out his hand, nothing in his manner to betray the warning in his eyes as they met hers. Reluctantly she surrendered her arm to him and he tucked it under his.

The sun was higher. A blackbird was perched on the wall serenading them. Jay Warwick had given way in the face of his aunt's eagerness for her plans, clearly unwilling to upset her by betraying his own displeasure. Everything should have been perfect. But that would have been too easy. She didn't think he would be quite so gentle with her, and her heart was pounding furiously as she was insistently propelled along a path dissecting the formal gardens, closely flanked by the tall, dangerous figure of her nemesis.

'There's really no need to escort me, Mr Warwick,' she said, finally breaking the silence. 'I'm sure I can find my own way.'

'I like to stretch my legs after a long drive.' He glanced sideways at her. 'I assure you I have no immediate plans to ravish you in the rhodedendrons.'

'It never occurred to me that you would,' she said. 'Unless of course the one-to-a-bed rule only applies *inside* the hall?'

'If you were considering putting it to the test, I would advise against it.'

'You're really quite safe, I promise,' she said flippantly, firmly ignoring the thought that if he had been intent on ravishment, she wasn't totally convinced that she would be able to resist him. It was infuriating.

He stopped, and she was forced to do the same. He regarded her thoughtfully, gold glints sparking in the depths of velvet brown eyes. 'Perhaps you should be more concerned for your own safety.' Then, ignoring her sharp intake of breath, he regained possession of her elbow and continued to propel her down a broad gravel path flanked on either side by the black skeletal shapes of ancient standard roses. This was hardly the pleasant walk in the garden that she had envisaged when she set out first thing. She attempted to shake free. But his grip was deceptively firm. 'I wouldn't want you to think, Kate, that because I have decided not to interfere with Tisha's plans I am happy about them.'

'I did get the hint of a feeling that you weren't too happy.'

'I believed I had scotched this particular bee in her bonnet. Presumably that's why she chose to go behind my back. She is a stubborn old woman and can't bear not to get her way. Clearly things are too far advanced to stop without causing her a great deal of distress. So be it.' He glanced at her. 'How long have you been here?'

'I arrived last night.'

'I see. Then you have very little time. I hope your much-vaunted powers of organisation are more than myth, because the house is opening in less than two weeks.'

'I know.'

'Well, it will keep you fully occupied. Not that there are many opportunities to flirt with the dinner guests here.'

Only the whiteness above her lip betrayed the effort it was taking Kate to keep her voice even, her expression bland. 'Perhaps I can have your assurance that the dinner guests won't flirt with me? Even those that live here?'

For a moment she thought she had taken him by surprise but he recovered so quickly that she couldn't be certain. 'At Fullerton Hall, Kate, I make the rules.'

She gave a little gasp. 'I have a few of my own and top of the list concerns — '

'You really are not in any position to dictate terms,' he interrupted, 'if there's a no-break clause in your contract.'

'Top of the list,' she repeated, furiously, 'concerns . . . ' This time there was no interruption, just the sudden certainty that she was about to make an utter fool of herself.

'Well?' he prompted, impatiently.

'It doesn't matter.' Insisting that he promise not to kiss her in the kitchen, or anywhere else for that matter, might just put ideas into his head regarding the simplest way to rid himself of her.

'This way, Kate.' He pushed open a pair of ornamental gates flanked by high formal yew hedges and guarded by a bronze wolf with a hungry leer. Jay patted the beast affectionately and then stepped through and on to the grassy path. Kate hesitated and he looked back.

' 'Enter these enchanted woods, you who dare.' Do you dare, Kate?'

She regarded him levelly. 'What could there possibly be to fear, Mr Warwick?'

In answer, he took her arm and led her along a narrow path knee-deep in bluebells. 'It's the possibility of danger that makes life interesting, Kate.' There was a resolute intensity about the man. 'We all need to take risks, or how will we know we are alive?'

He stopped and glanced down at her and frowned slightly. His arm was still linked in hers, holding her close on the narrow path, and above the heady scent of the flowers she could smell the warmth of his body, good cloth, leather. Every nerve-end was tingling, polarised by his presence, drawing her under his spell. Each moment this close to him was a risk and he was right. She could never remember feeling quite so vividly alive.

He continued to regard her for a moment with a slightly puzzled expression, then abruptly glanced at his watch. 'It's time to start work, Kate. You can begin by cooking me some breakfast.'

'You'd better take me back, then, Mr Warwick. I can't have you passing out from hunger in 'these enchanted woods'. It would be too bad if you were spirited away by a passing fairy.'

'There are things far more dangerous than fairies in the woods, Miss Thornley. Innocent-looking young women who look as if butter wouldn't melt in their mouths, for one.'

Kate felt the hot colour burning her cheekbones. 'How do you like your eggs?' she demanded, finally managing to wrench her arm from his. Presumably because he was no longer interested in holding it.

'Cooked,' he said, and smiled slightly. 'And on a plate, in case you had any more unconventional plans for them.' He opened the door for her and followed her into the kitchen. 'I'll eat in here. With you.'

Kate wrapped herself in an apron and went into the pantry for a bowl of eggs. 'Cooked on a plate,' she muttered angrily to herself. Kate put some bacon in a pan and placed it on the Aga rather firmly. Damn Jay Warwick, she thought angrily to herself, then applied herself to the task of providing the wretched man with breakfast. She added a couple of rashers of bacon to the pan. The early morning walk had sharpened her appetite and she smiled ruefully.

At least if she was eating it would give her something to do with her hands. Strangling the world's favourite bachelor wouldn't win her any friends on a jury. The door opened behind her but she made no indication that she heard, instead giving her total attention to the perfect execution of her eggs.

'That smells good.'

'I'm a very good cook.' She dished up the food and placed it on the table, marvelling at the steadiness of her hand. She met his eyes.

'I know. Sit down and eat your breakfast.' He pulled out a chair for her. He had capitulated so suddenly that she didn't quite believe it, and she hesitated. He regarded her steadily for a moment, then shrugged. 'If Tisha wants a teashop in the conservatory, Kate, she shall have it, but you're up against a deadline and you don't know your way about. It will take our combined efforts to make it work.'

'I wouldn't have thought you have much time to spare for such minor details.'

'In this case, I shall have to make the time. As soon as we've had breakfast we'll look at the conservatory and work out exactly what has to be done.'

They spent an hour in the conservatory and the time flew by as Jay listened intently to her ideas, his lateral manner of thinking offering solutions that might never have occurred to her.

'What are you going to do now?' he asked, as they made their way back to the kitchen in search of coffee.

'Write a shopping list and then let my fingers do the walking.'

'Don't you think you should consider a little market research?'

'Market research?'

'I normally employ a company to do it for me, but in this case I'm sure we could manage it between us.'

'And what will it entail?'

'A look at the opposition. There are a couple of tearooms in Oulton Market. I have to go out but I'll pick you up here at about a quarter to four.'

'But . . . ' He had already moved on. She hurried after him. 'Why don't you take your aunt?'

'My aunt employed you to advise her

and, since you are being paid handsomely for your expertise, I intend to take full advantage of your knowledge. Now if you'll excuse me I have some phone calls to make. I won't be in for lunch.' He didn't wait for her reply and she was left standing open-mouthed in the hall.

Catching sight of herself in a mirror, she shut her mouth quickly. 'Watch it, Kate,' she warned her reflection, and pulled a face at herself.

But in the event it hadn't been quite as bad as she had expected. Jay Warwick had a first-class business brain. His meteoric success in the cut-throat world of television was testament to that. And having made his decision to let her stay — and she was in no doubt that if he had wanted her to go he would have found a way to get rid of her — he had obviously decided to establish a reasonable working relationship. In the interests of keeping Tisha happy. She took herself off to the pantry to make an inventory of baking tins. It was a soothing, monotonous job, requiring total concentration.

★ ★ ★

'You're very quiet, Miss Thornley.' Jay Warwick changed gear as the road straightened and glanced across at her.

'I didn't realise I was expected to provide witty conversation as well as cook.'

'Only if you feel up to it.' He approached a tricky stretch of road and gave it his full attention and so missed the infuriated glance she threw at him. The road narrowed as it approached the small town of Oulton Market and Jay was forced to wait for a slow-moving tractor before he could park in the market square. Before she could release her seatbelt he was round the car and opening the door for her.

'Now,' he said, briskly, 'We have the Copper Kettle and Martha's Kitchen to choose from.' He indicated two tearooms that gleamed at one another across the square. 'Or should we try both?'

'Oh, in the interests of market research I'm sure we should. Although it might look a little odd.'

'And since presumably we'll have to eat something, it could also prove rather fattening.'

She allowed her eyes to drift down his lean figure. 'I don't think so. Unless you're trying to tell me that you run five miles a day and play squash three times a week?'

'I get the feeling you would relish the idea of my suffering, Kate. But you're quite right, I'm naturally skinny.'

'Fishing for compliments won't work with me, Mr Warwick. You already know what a very attractive man you are.'

'You're getting careless. That was almost a compliment.'

'Was it? I can assure you it wasn't meant to be.'

He was thoughtful for a moment. 'I begin to see why Tisha was impressed so with you. Which reminds me that she asked me to pick up a prescription for her.'

As they walked across the square to the chemist, Kate became increasingly aware that they were the centre of attention.

'You're attracting rather a lot of interest,' she said, finally.

'Not me. These people have known me all my life. You're the one arousing local curiosity. You're not quite my usual style, you see, so I'm afraid you'll be the subject of ill-informed speculation over dinner-tables throughout the parish tonight.' The idea did not appear to amuse him.

'I imagine you're referring to your famous weakness for leggy blondes? Surely they don't get invited to Fullerton Hall? The sleeping arrangements are somewhat restricted. And I would have thought they preferred to stay a little nearer the bright lights.'

'Would you?' He pocketed the prescription and turned an expressionless gaze upon her. Then a touch of derision touched his smile. 'The fortitude of some girls would probably

59

amaze you. They'll do anything to get on television. Even sleep alone.' She swallowed hard as he took her arm and headed for Martha's Kitchen. Apparently satisfied with the impression he had made, he handed her a menu. 'What can I offer you?'

Kate had not needed to look at the menu, using it only as a shield to recover her composure. 'A scone, please with fresh cream and raspberry jam.'

'Is that all?

'For the purposes of market research, Mr Warwick, it will do well enough.' The waitress brought their tea. 'I'll pour, shall I? I don't imagine you've had much experience with all those willing ladies eager to pander to your every whim.'

He bared his teeth at her as she poured two cups of tea. The waitress returned with their scones and Kate considered the offering.

Jay took the cup she handed to him and raised an enquiring brow as she broke the scone open, sniffed it, then pushed the plate away. 'Well?' he asked, slightly startled by this performance.

'This is a mass-produced scone. It could be purchased in a packet in any supermarket and will last for days.'

'Isn't that good?'

Kate propped her elbows on the table and leaned her face on her hands. 'That is a matter of opinion, Mr Warwick. But it isn't what Tisha has in mind, and if this is the kind of stuff you're prepared to offer your customers you certainly don't need me.'

Jay Warwick regarded her over the edge of his teacup. 'I thought we'd already established that.'

Kate stiffened. 'You don't give up, do you?' she said, furious with herself for being lulled into a false sense of security. If she was the one to crack, his aunt could hardly blame him.

He produced a note and, dropping it on the table, rose to his feet. 'How long do you think you will be able to stand it?'

'As long as you can dish it out,' she retorted.

His smile was grudging. 'Have you seen enough? Or should we check up on the Copper Kettle?'

'I'm sure that won't be necessary, Mr Warwick. At Fullerton Hall, as I'm sure you already know since you seem to be quite bright, you'll have a captive audience. And this place, at least, offers no incentive to escape.'

'That was nearly another compliment,' he said, a little brusquely, opening the car door for her. 'Aren't you afraid it will go to my head?'

Kate glanced up at him as she tucked her seatbelt into place. 'I'm sure an ego as large as yours can handle it.'

His eyes darkened and she saw with a sudden shock that she had made him angry. 'Damn you,' he said, and shut the door with rather more force than was necessary and turned away.

'Jay!'

He narrowed his eyes against the slanting sun and cursed softly under his breath. 'Hello, Mike.'

'I didn't realise you were home.' A

man, a little above average in height and with soft brown hair, hurried across the square towards them. He glanced in the car at Kate and then, pointedly, at Jay.

Jay performed perfunctory introductions. 'Kate Thornley, Mike Howard.'

Mike offered Kate his hand through the window. 'Hello, Kate,' he said warmly, his eyes riveted on her face.

She took the proffered hand and found it held firmly. 'Hello, Mike,' she said and swallowed a smile as a warning shadow crossed Jay Warwick's face.

'*Miss Thornley* is organising the catering at the house,' he said coolly. 'We're opening in a couple of weeks.'

'You've decided to go ahead, then?' Admiration lit the other man's eyes as he regarded Kate. 'Quite an undertaking. When's the big day? I shall certainly make an effort to be there.' He had addressed himself to Kate, but it was Jay who answered.

'It will be advertised.' He made an impatient move and Mike Howard reluctantly surrendered Kate's hand.

'I'd better let you get on, then. I'm sure you've a lot to do. I'll see you again soon, Kate.'

She smiled rather more warmly than she might normally have done as he waved and walked away across the square.

'He's the estate agent for the National Trust in this area,' Jay told her, as he climbed into the driving seat. 'In case you wanted to make a note.' There was something about the way he said it that made her look up.

'I might,' she said.

3

It was a breathless, angry drive back to the hall and it seemed only minutes before he slid to a halt alongside her van, still parked where she had left it when she arrived the evening before.

Kate moved to open the car door but Jay's hand detained her. For a moment she stared at his long fingers gripping her wrist with quite unnecessary force, then, suddenly furious with him, she flung up her arm, jerking free of his hold, and looked up. About to make a cutting remark, she was stopped in her tracks by the intensity of eyes gleaming with the hardness of agate.

'Behave yourself, Miss Thornley,' he advised her, in deadly earnest. 'This is a small community and I won't have Tisha embarrassed.'

'With you as a relation I should think that must be her permanent state of mind. Or are you so insensitive you don't even realise your public remarks about women might be considered offensive?' she came back at him, but if she thought he would be in the least disconcerted he immediately disillusioned her.

'The truth is often difficult to take,' he replied, and she was the one momentarily shaken by the utter conviction with which he spoke.

Whatever malicious quirk of fate had managed to twist her life in twelve short hours from one of comparative contentment to one of total disarray she had no way of knowing. But she was stuck with it. And so was Jay Warwick, and he needn't think she was going to lie down and let him walk all over her just because he had leapt to the wrong conclusion about her morals. It had been very easy to manage without the dubious comfort of a man in her life since breaking her engagement to David, but Jay Warwick had no right to dictate what she did with her private life. 'What I do when I'm not working is none of your business, Mr Warwick,' she told him. 'Just leave me to get on with what I'm paid for.'

'So long as that's all you get paid for,' he said harshly.

'How dare you?' Kate felt the colour flooding upwards from her neck. 'You are quite the most insufferable man it has ever been my misfortune to meet!'

His eyes sparked with gold lights. 'Is that so?' He leaned towards her. 'Well, you're going to have to learn to suffer, Miss Kate Thornley,' he said, slowly and carefully. 'I advised you to leave this morning. Perhaps you should have taken my advice while it was still possible. It's too late now.'

'Is it? Because you have to keep your aunt sweet in case she doesn't leave you all this?'

'Leave me . . . ?' His laugh was short and unpleasant. 'Dream on, sweetheart. I choose to keep Tisha *sweet*, as you so charmingly put it, because she gave up her own home to look after me when my mother jettisoned her responsibilities. Fullerton Hall, Kate, belongs to me.'

Kate felt the colour drain from her face as she absorbed the implication of his words. Trying desperately to keep her poise, she said, 'Then . . . I work for you?'

His tiger's eyes gleamed with satisfaction at the effect of this revelation. 'You work for me,' he confirmed. 'And I'll make it my business to remind you of that fact if you step out of line.'

'It would make life a whole lot easier if you would just stop . . . ' Kate faltered.

'Stop what?'

Tearing her up with his eyes. Making her aware of her body as no one had for years. The air between them seemed to vibrate with sexual tension. With a jolt, Kate quite suddenly knew exactly why Jason Warwick was so angry with her. She turned and fumbled desperately with the unfamiliar door-catch, urgently needing to get away from him. He was around the car in a moment to open the door for her, but he barred her escape, staring at her with a fierceness that chilled her.

'Please. Let me go.' His eyes narrowed at the sudden pleading in her voice. But he immediately stood back, releasing her, and she was out of the car before he could change his mind. But he hadn't quite finished with her.

'Since you are staying, Kate, perhaps you would be kind enough to put that heap — ' and he indicated her van ' — somewhere out of sight. There's plenty of room in the coach-house.'

Her hands shook as she searched for the keys in her bag. Eventually she found them and after considerable coaxing under his impassive gaze, the van finally relented and burst into noisy life. Her foot unsteady on the clutch, she hiccuped the vehicle rather jumpily into the shelter of the coach-house. She sat for a while within the safety of its hard-used frame, wishing it were possible just to drive away as far and as fast as she could and never look back. But she had committed herself.

And she had to be practical. She always had to be practical. She had nowhere to run to. She climbed from the van, eschewing the false security it seemed to offer. She had supplies to order, staff to find, far too much to do to worry about Jay Warwick. Yet as she worked in the little office in what had once been a butler's pantry, she was edgily aware of his presence in the house, jumpily certain that he would appear at her shoulder at any moment. It might almost have been a relief if he had, she decided in the end.

Nancy had laid three places in the small dining-room close to the kitchen that was used for all but the grandest occasions. Kate had queried it with the girl.

'It's Lady Maynard's orders, Miss Kate,' Nancy replied, and Kate had had to be content with that. But as the girl settled the tureen of soup on the table she couldn't help thinking that eating

with her young trainee at the kitchen
table would be altogether preferable.
Any pleasure in Fullerton Hall seemed
to have evaporated in the heat of Jay
Warwick's presence. She looked up as
the door opened and the man in
question entered the room.

Lady Maynard settled herself at the
table and shook out her napkin, asking
how she had spent her day, while Jay
opened a bottle of wine.

'Kate? Can I tempt you?'

'Thank you, Mr Warwick,' she said,
and he filled her glass.

'No need for such formality, Kate,'
Tisha Maynard, protested. 'Tell her to
call you Jay, darling. Everyone else
does.'

He regarded her steadily as she
ladled out hot soup. 'Kate can call me
by whatever name she chooses.' A glint
in his eyes suggested that he didn't
believe her choice was likely to be
anything as complimentary as his given
name.

Kate ladled piping hot soup into his

dish, fervently wishing it were his lap. 'Jay will be just fine,' she said, congratulating herself on her restraint.

Lady Maynard kept the conversation going, eager to hear how things were going, and Kate launched into an outline of the ideas that had already formed in her mind. Other than the occasional response to his aunt's eager prompting, he added little to the discussion, but she was conscious of him listening, watching her, every moment.

Afterwards she declined an invitation to join Tisha in the drawing-room for coffee, retiring instead to her office to continue the detailed planning, now that the broad strokes were in place. She was reading through a series of lists, double checking, when she suddenly became conscious of being watched. She looked up to find Jay standing in the doorway and regarding her with something approaching amusement.

'Do you normally become so engrossed in what you're doing?' he asked.

She flushed, only too aware of her

habit of muttering out loud when she was planning anything. 'How long have you been standing there?' she demanded.

'Quite long enough.' His unexpected laughter was disconcerting. It made him seem too human. 'I was rather hoping you would be making some coffee.'

Kate glanced at her watch, a very large one with cartoon characters on the face, bought for her birthday by Sam. 'It's rather late for coffee.'

He followed her glance and for a moment his eyes rested upon the watch and his eyebrows rose slightly. 'I would have thought that was for me to say.'

She shrugged. If he couldn't sleep, that was his problem. 'Can I make something for Tisha?'

'She has already gone to bed.'

'Oh.' She suddenly felt very alone with Jay Warwick in Fullerton Hall. Alone in the small circle of light thrown over her desk by the lamp that left the rest of the room in darkness, and it was a relief to have something positive to do, an excuse to escape such close confinement with him. She stood up and waited for him to move so that she could pass without touching him. For a moment he remained where he was, challenging her almost to risk bodily contact. Then, when she didn't move, he stepped back, an ironical smile twisting his lips. She found a mug and spooned in instant coffee, quickly wiping up a few grains that had unaccountably missed their target.

He took the mug she offered, but instead of disappearing as she had hoped, he followed her back to the office and lodged himself on the table and picked up the list she had been working on. 'Will we really need all this?'

Happy to keep his mind on business, she nodded. 'And more. Do you have an account with a food wholesaler?'

He raised a dark brow. 'We don't normally eat in this quantity. No doubt one can be arranged.'

'The sooner the better. They'll want to check your credit rating.'

'Will they? I think you'll find my name will be sufficient to guarantee my credit. I'll sort it out tomorrow.' Jay's leg swung nonchalantly. 'Will that be soon enough?'

'If that's the earliest you can manage, it will have to be,' she replied coolly.

He raised an unsettling smile. 'I'm going to take Tisha's idiotic dog for a walk before I go to bed. I don't suppose you'd care to join me?'

For the walk or in bed? She coloured as the thought jumped unbidden into her mind. 'No,' she said. Then, aware that she had been abrupt, she added a reluctant, 'Thank you.'

He bowed slightly. 'I'll say goodnight, then, Kate.'

'Goodnight, Jay.' And she made sure she was upstairs in her own room with the door shut long before he returned.

She opened her diary and noted with a slight shock that copy was due for her cookery column in the *Evening Mail*. The days were flying by at a ridiculous speed.

When she had told the woman's page editor that she would be in the country for a few months, she had suggested that Kate take the opportunity to try something rather different from her usual straightforward dinner party recipes. Easy enough to agree to write a country diary on the spur of the moment, she thought, pulling her portable typewriter out of the cupboard where she had stowed it, looking around for somewhere to work.

She cleared a space on her dressing-table, rolled in a clean sheet of paper and stared at it blankly. Nothing had happened. She corrected that thought. Nothing had happened that she could possibly write about.

Tentatively she began to type. She began with her first impressions of the house in the hope that something might spark an idea. She heard Daisy's paws scuffling up the oak staircase that led from the hall, followed by the crisp step of Jay Warwick. She sensed rather than heard him pause outside her door and she stopped typing, uneasily wondering if she had remembered to lock it. The footsteps continued and she stared at what she had written in despair. Hopeless. She tore the sheet out of the machine and crumpled it up. She decided to write to Sam instead.

Half a page into her letter the idea hit her. She abandoned Sam's letter to finish another time and began to write. 'Dear cousin Kate,' she wrote. 'I am writing to tell you about a new position I have taken in the country with a gentleman by the name of — ' she paused and searched her brain for a suitable pseudonym ' — Mr Jack Wessex. He has a house in London as well, so you may have met him since he appears to be quite *fond* of cooks. At least he was most friendly to me when he came into the kitchen . . . '

★   ★   ★

A good night's sleep put everything into perspective. Writing her 'Letter from a

Country Kitchen' had proved a safety valve. Poking a little fun, however anonymously, at Jay Warwick had released the tension, allowing her to see the ridiculous side of the situation. The fact that he would never know hardly mattered, and doubtless he would be returning to London within a day or two. Now she was eager to meet the challenge that Tisha Maynard had given her.

And she seemed to be proved right, since his mind seemed firmly set on business when he emerged from his study shortly before ten. 'Kate, I've organised a wholesaler for you. If you're ready I'll take you there now.'

'There's no need,' she said. He glanced at her and she realised that she had sounded less than grateful. 'I can't believe it's quite your cup of tea.'

'Your belief is well-founded. But you don't know where it is and I have to go into Norwich anyway.'

'In that case I'll follow you in the van.' He didn't argue and she fetched her bag and crossed to the coach-house. There was an empty space where she had parked it. Nonplussed, she looked about her. It couldn't have been stolen. Who on earth would take it when there were four other vehicles, all gleaming expensive motors, parked alongside? Then she knew and angrily turned to confront the undoubted author of its disappearance.

He was framed for a moment in the doorway, his hands jammed tightly in his pockets as he regarded her confusion. He had referred to himself as skinny, but he was far from that, Kate thought. A pair of faded jeans clung to strong well muscled legs and stretched tightly across his hips, and his wide, square shoulders blocked out more than his fair share of the sun. He held himself with the ease and assurance of someone comfortable with his own body and he moved towards her now with a careless grace that made her want to scream.

'Where is it?' She felt that her restraint deserved a medal.

'I had the garage tow it away. It is

clearly in need of a serious service.'

'Possibly,' she acceded. 'And when I can afford it, it will have one.'

'While you work for me you're my responsibility, Kate, and I insist that any vehicle you use on my business is totally roadworthy. Is it properly insured for business use?'

'Of course it is.'

'There's nothing to worry about then. Don't fret, it'll be back tomorrow.'

'That's wonderful. So how am I going to get to the wholesaler's now?'

'You're coming with me. I thought we had already established that.' He flickered a glance at her that might have twitched into a smile given the slightest encouragement. None was forthcoming. 'In the Range Rover.' He led the way to the silver monster at the far end and opened the door. It was a long way up and, before she could haul herself in, his hands were around her waist and he had lifted her effortlessly on to the seat.

'Thank you,' she said, stiffly.

'Any time,' he said. 'I'm sure the pleasure was entirely mine,' he added, with a touch of wry humour that took her by surprise.

He drove with total concentration and she was grateful that he found it unnecessary to cover the silence between them with pointless chatter and she was able to concentrate on the strange, rich farmland that they passed with deceptive swiftness in the smooth silence of the Rover. She glanced at the dashboard. Her poor van would have been shaking uncontrollably at such speed. It seemed very little time before they had reached the outskirts of the city and he pulled up before a building in the industrial area. 'How long are you likely to be?'

'An hour at the most.'

He nodded. 'I won't keep you waiting.' True to his word, he was in the car park when she emerged and he opened the door and jumped down.

As she made for the passenger seat, Jay stopped her. 'Would you care to drive back?' He offered her the keys. She itched to get her hands on the beautiful machine, but was instantly suspicious of his motives.

'Why?'

'If you can get us home safely I'll let you out in the Rover on your own. I won't always be around to drive you.'

'Is that a promise?' she demanded. He grinned and she had to remind herself very firmly of the resolution she had made not to say the first thing that came into her head every time he infuriated her. 'My van will be back from the garage tomorrow,' she added carefully.

'Only if it passes the mechanic's inspection.'

She snatched the keys and he laughed as he lifted her into the seat. Crossly she fitted the keys into the ignition, certain she had made a grave mistake but unable to fathom the reason for her unease. Except that she was doing what he wanted. Her fingers were shaking slightly as she started the engine and drove carefully out into the road, feeling her way through the controls.

'It's a relief to see that you don't always drive like a kangaroo,' Jay said, as they approached a junction.

'I never drive like a kangaroo,' she protested, missed a gear, and the engine roared furiously.

'You were saying?' he prompted, when she had finally sorted herself out and they were moving smoothly forward once more.

She didn't rise to the bait, but negotiated a round-about with excessive care, before picking up speed as she gained more confidence, enjoying the power of the big machine.

Jay glanced at his watch. 'Turn left here'.

She complied. 'Where are we going?'

'We have an appointment.'

'We?'

'Yes, we. The two of us. For lunch. Here we are. Park over there.' Kate pulled up in the car park of a long sprawling country pub, but left the engine running.

Jay leaned across, switched off the

engine and pocketed the keys before she realised what he was at. 'Mustn't leave the engine running when you park. Now, shall we have some lunch?'

'I don't think so.'

He jumped down and walked around to open her door. 'You might as well join me, because you're not going anywhere until I've eaten.' He reached out, grasped her waist and lifted her down before she could protest further.

'This is kidnapping,' she exclaimed, trying very hard to ignore the warmth of his hands around her waist and the fact that every cell and sinew seemed to jump to attention and salute at his touch.

'Is it? Well, in that case I may as well be hung for a sheep as a lamb.' He jerked her close. 'I've been promising myself this all morning.' She was quite unprepared for the impact of his mouth on hers, the flood of excitement that sent her blood racing and pounding through her veins. It was a long time since anyone had seriously kissed her. And Jay Warwick was a serious kisser.

Totally oblivious of her surroundings and the warning klaxon hammering in her head that she had to stop him, Kate responded, quite powerless to help herself.

There was nothing rushed or superficial about the way his lips teased hers apart. Kate stood very still as Jay's hand slid over her back, pressing her close to him, forcing her to acknowledge his dominance as he leaned over her, his tongue moving in a slow, sensuous, irresistible exploration of her mouth. Only the sound of another car being driven into the car park, and the door being slammed, shockingly roused her to her senses.

Lifting his head, Jay regarded her with insolent amusement from under heavy lids. 'Now,' he said matter-of-factly as he released her, 'sue me. But after lunch.'

She gasped. 'You . . . '

He didn't wait to hear what she was going to call him. Instead he grasped her elbow and led her firmly into a low oak-beamed bar and sat her, none too gently, at a table. 'What would you like to drink?' he asked, his eyes challenging her to make a scene.

'An orange juice,' she replied rather more faintly than she had intended, still numb from the shock of his kiss. It was true then. She hadn't imagined the look in his eyes the evening before. He didn't like her any more than she liked him, but he wanted her. And she had the feeling that whatever Jay Warwick wanted, he had. She didn't care what he had said about his sleeping arrangements in Norfolk. He wanted her. How or why were pointless questions. And to tell herself that it didn't matter, because she could easily resist him, was madness.

Tentatively she raised her fingers to her throbbing mouth, jumping as he placed her drink in front of her and sat down.

'I've brought you the menu, but I'd recommend the crab.'

'That would be lovely,' she replied dully, not looking. She had no interest in food. She had to stop him. Make absolutely certain he didn't kiss her ever again. But how?

'You're so difficult to please.' She looked up to find him regarding her thoughtfully. Why wouldn't he stop? Just leave her alone and go back to London where there were a dozen women who would be glad to warm his bed. Until she had met him she had been contented, known exactly where she was. But now?

'I don't normally eat lunch.' she said, and looked up, determined not to let him see her confusion. She was twenty-three, with a career and responsibilities, too old to be putty in any man's hands. Good grief, he probably kissed dozens of girls a week. That was why he was so good at it.

She opened the menu, studying it carefully, but, despite the stiff mental talking-to she had given her libido, the words remained a meaningless jumble.

'Well?' he asked finally.

'The crab will be lovely.' She sipped the orange juice and looked around. Anywhere but at Jay Warwick. 'This is a lovely old place,' she said in the light conversational tone one would use with a stranger.

'Quite lovely.' She glanced sharply at him. His expression was unexceptional, but she had the feeling that she had missed something. He always seemed to be saying just a little bit more than the words implied. The waitress arrived for their order and Kate noted the sudden stillness about the girl as he smiled.

'Would you mind signing the menu for me, Mr Warwick?' she breathed. He obliged, asking the girl her name and putting her at her ease, making her laugh.

He had never made any attempt to put *her* at her ease, Kate thought. On the contrary, he seemed to go out of his way to keep her off balance. Yet he had insisted that she stay. And stay she would, although every fibre of her being screamed at her to run for cover before he turned her life upside down.

But there was Sam. Always Sam. And Kate knew that she would never again have the opportunity to save so much money so quickly. It was the one reason she had been willing to leave London. With the money from the flat and this job she was sure she could persuade the bank to back her in a small restaurant. All she had to do was keep her head for six months. Not even that. Jay Warwick would have to return to London soon. His business was there.

The thought was reassuring, and by the time their food arrived her emotions were firmly back in line and she was able to give it her full attention.

'You should eat lunch more often, Kate. It apparently agrees with you.' He was leaning back in his chair, watching her.

'The food was excellent. Thank you.'

'Jay.'

'I beg your pardon?'

'Thank you, Jay. I want you to use my name.'

'Oh, I see.' She bowed graciously. 'Thank you, Jay.'

'That's better. Coffee?'

She shook her head and glanced at her watch. 'I really must get back.'

'Coffee?' he repeated.

She smiled brightly to cover the sudden spurt of anger. 'No, thank you, *Jay*. I do have a great deal to do and time is getting on.'

'Of course.' He made no move to leave. Instead he reached across the table and took her hand. She wanted to pull it away. Every vibrating inch of her screamed to her to pull her hand away from his grasp. But she allowed him to hold her fingers firmly but gently in his own, forcing herself to relax, not betray by one twitch how his touch was affecting her.

'I find your taste in wristwatches interesting,' he said. 'May I see?'

She reluctantly surrendered her wrist and he examined the watch.

'Most amusing.'

'Sam gave it to me for my birthday,' she said, instantly defensive.

'Sam?' he asked. 'Who is Sam?'

She realised with a start that he had

misunderstood. She had begged for a solution to her problem. He had presented her with one. 'Sam and I live together,' she said.

'You live together? A very loose sort of arrangement, surely? Doesn't he mind you flashing your beautiful eyes at every man you see?'

'Apparently not. We've been together for three years.'

'Sam,' he said, derisively, 'is a fool. And very cheap.'

Kate reclaimed her wrist. 'When someone loves you, money doesn't matter.'

'Or fidelity apparently. And what does Sam think about you spending six months in the wilds of Norfolk, I wonder?'

'I needed a job.'

'The man's an idiot to let you out of his sight.'

She stood up, pleased with the effect of her little deception. 'Not an idiot,' she said, unaware that her voice had softened. 'The dearest, kindest . . . '

Her voice trailed into silence. She had nearly said sister and that would spoil everything.

He unfolded from his seat. 'I get the picture, Kate. No need to labour it. He's the only man in your life.'

'You've got it in one, Mr . . . Jay.'

'Then the next time I kiss you, Kate, I'm sure you'll be able to convince me of that,' he drawled.

She flamed. 'There isn't going to be a next time.' And she walked quickly out of the pub and was sitting in the driver's seat of the Rover when he emerged.

He handed her the keys. 'Drive carefully, sweetheart.'

She didn't bother to query this instruction. He was simply being flippant. Nevertheless, she took his advice to heart and drove with extra care back to Fullerton Hall. Not for Jay Warwick. If she had thought she could turn him to jelly by driving at speed through the country lanes she would have done it with the greatest pleasure.

But her own nerves were in such rags that she needed all the careful concentration she could muster to take her mind off her disturbing passenger.

When she pulled up in the yard, she jumped quickly down to avoid the indignity of him lifting her, to avoid the unsettling closeness and his hands clasped tightly around her waist. His smile as he joined her was knowing.

She felt suddenly awkward. 'Thank you for the lunch.'

'Any time, Kate. I enjoyed myself. I particularly enjoyed kissing you. And you enjoyed that too, I could tell.'

'Damn you, Jay Warwick! Damn you to hell!'

'Too late, my dear. Years too late for that.' He stepped back, allowing her to escape, his provoking laughter following her into the house.

She fled to her room and splashed her face with cold water. Gradually the shaking subsided and she began to get a hold on herself.

There were several calls during the

afternoon from suppliers hoping to drum up a little business, and they were put through to the kitchen with increasing irritation by Jay.

Once they were settled down over the dinner-table he brought the matter up. 'I'll have to have another line put in the study, Tisha. Opening up the house is interfering with business.'

'Do whatever you like, Jay. You usually do.' Lady Maynard turned to Kate. 'Talking of telephones reminds me that there was a call for you today, Kate, when you were out. I'm so sorry, I should have told you before.'

'I don't suppose it was important,' she said, but her nerves jumped to attention.

'On the contrary. I rather believe it was. It was from Sam.'

Kate felt herself go pale. It was always the same. Ever since the crash she had dreaded the unexpected telephone call. 'Sam? What is it? Has there been an accident?'

Tisha Maynard looked up in surprise

at her agitation. 'No, dear. Nothing like that. It was simply a request that you send a hundred pounds. As quickly as possible.'

A contemptuous hiss from the other side of the table jerked her head up. Jay was staring at her, his mouth twisted into a hard mocking smile.

'Perhaps he'll use it to buy you a decent watch,' he said with quiet venom. She didn't move and he waved her away. 'Hadn't you better run along? If it's urgent?'

'It'll wait,' she said coldly. She couldn't imagine what her sister needed a hundred pounds for. However urgent it was, she would have to sweat it out for another half-hour. She picked up a spoon, but Jay reached across the table and grasped her wrist.

'I insist, Kate. Go now. You shouldn't keep the man waiting.'

Tisha Maynard's brows rose some-what dramatically. She knew exactly who Sam was, had invited her to spend half-term with them. But when she turned to Kate to share the joke, she caught the silent plea in Kate's eyes. She glanced at her nephew and a mischievous glint sparked in her eye.

'Such a charming young man,' she remarked, without a blush. 'Do give him my apologies, Kate, for not passing on his message sooner.'

'Thank you, Tisha.' They exchanged a look and the older woman nodded slightly. 'I'll go now, if you'll excuse me.'

'Of course. Do let her go Jay, you're quite bruising the poor girl's wrist.'

She rang from the kitchen phone, her fingers shaking at having stooped to such deception and, worse, having involved Tisha Maynard. She had no idea how she could explain. But as soon as she heard Sam's voice her dismay was momentarily pushed to one side.

'A bike!' Her laugh was a little shaky. 'Couldn't you have written instead of sending a life-or-death message?'

'Sorry. It's just that mine is really past it and it would make life so much easier. Several of the girls are after it, you see, and if I could say the cheque's in the post . . . '

'But I was going to buy you a new one for Christmas!' Kate protested.

'This one will do just fine, honestly!' There was an almost comical pleading in her voice that made Kate laugh.

'All right, darling, if you must have it I'll send the cheque first thing in the morning.' She hung up and, still laughing, turned to see Jay standing in the doorway.

'Emergency over, I take it?' he asked evenly.

4

'So it's true. You actually give him money.' His lip curled in distaste.

She had no one but herself to blame for his misreading of the situation and if she hadn't been so vexed, if it hadn't hurt quite so much to see the disdain in his eyes, she might just have given way to her first instinct to blurt out the truth.

'Of course I give him money,' she retorted, casually, abandoning any effort not to refer to Sam as 'he'. It had gone too far for that. But she would stick to the truth as far as she could. 'Sam needs a lot of support. I'm happy to help . . . ' She faltered as he took a step towards her, his hands clenched as if he wanted to grab her and shake her and was having the greatest difficulty in stopping himself.

'Perhaps if you stopped propping him

up, he'd manage to stand on his own two feet.'

Kate's eyes flew open, startled by the harshness in his voice. He was deadly serious. A little scared now by the fierceness of his reaction, she said, 'Sam's feet are quite adequately exercised.' She turned away, signalling that as far as she was concerned the conversation was at an end.

He caught her shoulder and turned her back to face him. 'You keep him, don't you? That's why you needed this job.' His eyes were black with disbelief. 'Has he promised to repay you when he makes his fortune?'

'Sam repays me in ways you cannot begin to imagine,' she retaliated fervently. The explosive nature of his response made his assumption of the method of repayment all too clear and the colour flooded to her cheeks. How on earth had she ever got herself into such a ridiculous situation? She had invented a man in her life to keep Jay Warwick at a distance and now they were *arguing* about him! She was seized by something that could easily have been a fit of the giggles, but she was very much afraid that it might just become hysteria.

But he hadn't finished with her. Any thought of laughter, no matter what kind, vanished as his eyes raked her body. He was suddenly closer without having seemed to move, but Kate defiantly stood her ground and for a moment the tension was thick enough to cut. Then very slowly he lifted his hand and lightly drew a well-shaped thumb down the length of her jaw, and she shuddered. 'You should know, Kate, that a girl who looks like you doesn't have to pay for her pleasure. And he can't be *that* special, can he, since you're always so eager in someone else's arms?' She had backed herself into a situation from which, even if it had been possible, she no longer wished to escape. His insult had gone too deep for that. She no longer cared that she had deliberately deceived him. 'Shall I remind you?' His knuckles grazed her overheated cheek and he moved closer so that he was almost, but not quite, touching her.

Kate jerked her head back, breaking the insidious contact before it entirely sapped her will to resist and she was begging him to do anything he wanted. She stepped sharply back, turned and put the length of the kitchen between them before she spoke. 'I don't need reminding of anything,' she said. 'If you have something to say to me that concerns my work, I'll listen. If not, perhaps you'll be good enough to leave me in peace.'

'Kate?' He had followed her and she spun around, startled at the closeness of his voice in her ear. But his expression was cloaked, anger and smouldering desire concealed behind a bland mask that gave away nothing, except perhaps for a disquieting glint in his eyes.

'Well?' she demanded, aggression covering the imperative of her own desire.

'On the subject of work.' He waited

for her response.

'Work?' It was the last thing she had expected. 'What about work?'

'I understand from Tisha that you agreed to cook for any dinner parties she decided to hold during your stay here.'

'Yes,' Kate affirmed. 'I did. Has she made some plans?'

'No. But I've decided to invite an old friend to dinner.'

'Just one?'

'One is quite enough. Next Saturday — the night before we open the hall. We'll eat in the dining-hall. She'll enjoy that.'

With one hand he offered seduction, with the other he ordered dinner for another girl. She wondered which of his glamorous companions was being honoured by a visit to the ancestral home. The sharp green jab of jealousy was unexpected, ridiculous in the circumstances, but no less painful.

'And will she be staying for breakfast?'

He smiled, very slightly. 'I hardly think that's any of your business, Kate but no. She lives near enough for me to take her home.'

'How convenient. No stains on the sheets to shock the staff.' Under his ominious calm she managed to get a grip on her emotions. 'Have you any preference for the menu?'

'None whatever. I'll leave that entirely to you.' He turned to leave, but paused in the doorway. 'Except that Annabel hates fish.' Annabel Courtney. An old friend indeed. He had been squiring her for as long as she could remember. There had been numerous rumours of something more permanent, but nothing ever came of it.

'No oysters, then?' she murmured, and jumped as the kitchen door banged shut behind him.

*　*　*

Jay retired to his study to work with instructions that he was not to be disturbed, rarely appearing for meals, preferring to eat from a tray at his desk. Unfortunately, Kate thought as she responded in Nancy's absence to yet another demand for coffee, it was a one-way transaction. On Thursday evening, however, he called her into the study.

He was writing at his desk, isolated in a yellow circle of light thrown by a tall lamp at his elbow. The only other illumination in the room was from a log fire burning in the hearth, its flames reflecting in the tall windows opposite

'You wanted to see me, Jay?'

As he looked up she thought he looked tired. 'Hello, Kate. Sit down.' He threw a pair of gold-rimmed spectacles on to the desk in front of him and rubbed his eyes. 'How are things going?'

'No problems,' she said briskly, lowering herself into a chair in front of the desk, determined to keep the interview on a strictly impersonal level. It was the first time they had exchanged more than the barest civilities since their angry exchange in the kitchen. She told herself she preferred it that way.

'Good.' He sat back and stared at her for a moment, a slight frown creasing his forehead.

Discomfited by his scrutiny, Kate made a move. 'If there's nothing else I do need to get on.'

'You seem to be working very long hours.'

'Only now, while I'm getting the systems into place. Once things are running it will be a lot easier. You've been working long hours too.'

'There's no comparison. You have no personal stake in the Conservatory, Kate, whereas I am about to invest several million pounds in a new venture. A few hours ensuring that the figures are correct is a sound investment of my time.'

'Surely you have accountants to do that for you?'

'Yes, I have accountants. Talented,

hard-working, all of them. But it's my money. It makes my eye that little bit keener.'

'Yes,' she said, a little ruefully. 'The balancing act between profit and loss is a precarious one. It has a magic way of concentrating the mind.'

'Business was tough? Is that why you took Tisha's offer?'

'Partly,' she said, and left it at that.

He didn't enquire further, but rose, stretched, then moved across to the sideboard and poured himself a scotch. He turned to her. 'What will you have?'

'Nothing, thank you. I really do have a lot of work, Jay.'

'This is work, I promise. But I'd rather sit by the fire with you and discuss it over a drink. I've been stuck behind that desk all day. Consider it an alternative tea-break.' He offered her a smile. 'I'm quite sure you deserve it.'

She kept her eyes cast down, apparently absorbed in the rich detail of the carpet. 'If you put it that way, I'll have a small gin with a lot of tonic.'

He poured the drink and carried it across to a pair of old high-backed leather chairs that flanked the stone hearth. 'Come and sit over here, it's more comfortable.' Reluctantly she moved to the chair and perched on the edge of the seat, took the proffered glass and sipped.

He sat opposite her and stretched his long legs towards the fire. 'I love log fires. I really miss this when I'm in London.'

'The nights are still chilly,' she agreed, and could have bitten off her tongue for sounding so ridiculously prim.

He glanced across at her. 'Relax, Kate. I'm not going to jump on you.'

'That will make a change.' She caught herself. Keep to business, she reminded herself. 'What exactly do you want to discuss?' she asked.

'Last-minute details. Even the smallest ventures need a little care if they are to succeed.' His eyes flickered over her rigid body. 'When you sit back and relax, we'll begin.' He took a long draught of whisky and stretched out a foot to prod the logs, which flared into life, throwing a sudden heat on to her face. She continued to sit stubbornly upright for a while, but he made no further attempt to talk to her and it became apparent that he meant precisely what he said. Feeling rather silly, she shifted slightly, allowed her limbs to relax against the old leather and stretched her toes towards the fire. It was . . . pleasant.

He gave no indication that he had noticed her capitulation and for a while she wondered if he had forgotten that she was there. The movement of the flames was oddly hypnotic, their warmth making her limbs heavy, languorous.

When he spoke she physically jumped. 'I'd like to try a dummy run in the Conservatory tomorrow afternoon,' he said. He drained his glass and glanced across at her, but his face was devoid of any expression that might give her a clue to his thoughts. 'Can you manage it?'

If I don't sleep for the next twenty-four hours, she thought, mentally chiding herself for allowing him to lull her into so false a sense of security. On top of the distraction of his dinner with Annabel Courtney, training a group of local sixth-form girls to wait at tables and the slow wind-up to the sheer physical effort involved in the preparation of food in quantity, this was clearly meant to be the last straw. 'It's an excellent idea,' she said.

He regarded her thoughtfully. 'I'm full of good ideas.'

'Where will you get your customers from?'

He shrugged. 'My publicity people have been drumming up a little interest with their contacts. I've been bombarded with requests for a preview from the local press, and one or two of the national papers are prepared to give us some coverage too. If I give them the grand tour and you provide the afternoon tea we should be home and dry.'

'Will the television people be coming?'

Jay's face became still. 'Why do you ask?' His voice was low and even, but his eyes were watchful, suspicious almost.

'I just wondered. It seems likely, since you're in the medium. Or would the opening of any other country house warrant quite such flattering interest?'

'Why do you want to know?' he asked again.

'I ought to get my hair done,' she said, somewhat flippantly, since she didn't have a moment to spare.

'Ah!' The sound was a long velvet sigh. He stood up and took her glass, refilling it without bothering to ask if she wanted another. 'If you fancy yourself as a TV cook, my dear, you're not going the right way about it.'

'Oh? And what is the right way?'

His eyes were dark and unreadable in the shifting firelight. 'Come to my room tonight, Kate, and I'll show you.' He held out her glass and she took it, her insides flipping over as their fingers touched.

Kate took a quick drink, anything to hide the sudden hunger kindled by his words, the simple need to stretch out her hand and touch him. If he ever guessed how hard she had to fight the burning attraction that the mere sight of him engendered he would take everything he wanted. Take it and leave her an empty husk. At least when David had broken their engagement she had retained the cold comfort of her self-respect.

With a tremendous effort of will she managed to look puzzled. 'Surely that would be breaking the house rules?'

'It's my house. They're my rules.'

She swallowed. 'A television series was suggested to me quite recently, as a matter of fact. On that occasion I was invited to a party to discuss it. But I have a feeling that the end result was supposed to be the same.' She looked straight at him. 'It's a very odd way to do business.'

'It has a long provenance, Kate, dating from the time the first cave-woman found it was the easiest way to get a meal.'

'I imagine she was the one with her

back on the rock and she had to do the cooking. Not entirely a one-way transaction.'

'But a great deal easier than catching a woolly mammoth. Who was it?'

'Who . . . ?'

'Who tried to tempt you into bed with a TV series? I warn you, not everyone in the business is the soul of probity.'

'Do you mean,' she asked, with every appearance of horror, 'that he might not have been quite *serious*?'

His eyes flickered over her. 'I'm sure he was very serious about the bed part. I rather doubt you would ever have seen the inside of a television studio.'

'You shock me, Jay. How fortunate that I couldn't take the man up on his offer. Sam . . . ' Sam had been dancing that night, a small solo in her school show. She wouldn't have missed it, even if she had believed in the television series.

He abruptly turned away. 'It isn't necessary to explain.' His eyes had lost their warmth. Lost all expression. 'May I take it that you can cope tomorrow?'

She placed her glass, barely touched, on the table beside her and rose somewhat shakily to her feet and walked to the door. The truce was apparently over. 'You may. But if you have any idea of the numbers involved it would be a help.'

He didn't turn around. 'You won't know how many people to expect on Sunday. It will make it more realistic.'

★　★　★

The journalists and film crews arrived just after lunch on Friday and Jay showed them around the house before delivering them to the head gardener for a tour of the grounds.

'Is everything ready?' His appearance in the kitchen caused a quiver amongst the excited seventeen-year-olds who had been given the afternoon off school for the occasion at Jay's special request. Normally they would only work on

Sunday afternoons. She nodded. 'We're ready.'

She was buttering the umpteenth batch of teacakes when the door opened and she was confronted with a camera and a microphone.

An interviewer, vaguely familiar, chatted for a few minutes, asking her about herself and her job, while she continued to work. She was too busy to feel nervous and it was only later, when Tisha asked her if she wished to watch the local evening magazine programme, that she felt a sudden qualm about how she had performed. She immediately dismissed her nerves as ridiculous. They wouldn't use the footage from the kitchen when there was so much else to show.

There were establishing shots of the outside of Fullerton Hall and Jay, completely at home before the cameras, telling a little of its history.

Kate leaned forward when the camera panned the Conservatory, pleased to see how attractive the new green linen looked against the white wrought iron. Then she drew in a sharp breath as she saw herself chatting quite casually about how everything was freshly made, piling the teacakes on to a plate.

'Very professional, Kate,' Jay said, a cutting edge to his voice. 'I think we'll be overrun on Sunday. Everyone will want to meet the cook. It's rather a pity the kitchen is out of bounds. I recorded the programme — would you like a copy to keep? You never know when it might come in useful.'

'Thank you, Jay.' She took the barb buried in the offer and hurled it back. 'I'm sure Sam would love to see it.'

★ ★ ★

On Saturday afternoon Jay wandered into the kitchen and stood for a while watching her prepare the food for his intimate little dinner party. She tried to ignore him, devoting her entire attention to the preparation of her choux pastry.

He watched her for a while in silence, then said, 'How's Sam?' She continued to stir the mixture in the saucepan. 'Did he get his cheque safely?'

Kate gave him a sideways glance. 'I imagine so. Although what business it is of yours I don't know.'

'He didn't ring to say thank you?' he persisted. She didn't answer. Couldn't trust herself to. 'No. Well, if you sponge off young women, good manners aren't going to have a very high priority in your life, I suppose.'

'What's your excuse, Jay?' she asked, without taking her eyes off the careful blending of her ingredients.

'I had a deprived childhood.'

'You don't know the meaning of the word.' Kate removed the saucepan from the hob and added an egg, beating it with a practised action that was as automatic as breathing.

'Don't I?'

She gave an angry little shrug, thinking of Sam, all she had lost. But she kept it to herself. She added

116

another egg to the mixture and carried on beating. 'I imagine if it hadn't arrived I would have heard by now,' she said. In a way it was a great deal easier when he was being deliberately unpleasant. That way she knew exactly where she stood. She raised her lashes and regarded him steadily. 'I've no doubt that he'll thank me very nicely when he sees me.' A third egg was added and, if the beating had become a little ragged, only she noticed.

'No doubt,' he said, his voice pregnant with meaning. 'Kate . . . ?'

'Yes?' She surprised a perplexed expression that deepened the lines grooved into his cheeks.

He shook his head. 'Nothing.' With that he removed himself from the kitchen.

Half an hour later the phone rang. 'A call for you,' Jay said, brusquely. It was her editor.

'Kate, darling? Who on earth was that who answered the phone? He was barely civil.'

'It's not a very good time, Lorna. We're all up to our eyes — '

'Sorry, sweetie. I won't keep you. I just wanted you to know how much we all loved your 'Letter From a Country Kitchen'.'

'Oh, good.' She had been so busy that she hadn't had time to wonder.

'Very original.' She paused. 'Could you produce it weekly, instead of fortnightly? I could run it again this week.'

Kate stifled a little stab of something close to guilt. 'I'll try, Lorna. Look, I must go. Something's about to boil over.' She hung up. She was torn between delight at this unexpected success and something close to panic. Suppose Lorna had realised who Jay was when he answered the phone. It was hardly fair . . .

The phone rang again and she picked it up. 'I'm not your answering service, Kate,' Jay said coldly, before she could speak. 'It's Mike Howard. Tell him you're busy! I need the phone.' She stared at the receiver. This was the man she had been worried about being fair to? Lorna could have her copy as soon as she found a moment to write it. And when Mike Howard asked her out for a meal one day the following week, she said yes with an immediacy that must have flattered him.

Afterwards she regretted it. It was just an added complication to a life already in chaos, but she had too much to do without worrying about her motives in accepting his invitation. He was pleasant enough. An evening out would probably do her good.

By nine-thirty the dinner had been served. Only the dessert remained, and Nancy came to the kitchen with the disquieting request from Jay that Kate should take it up to the dining-room herself. It hadn't been enough that she had cooked for this woman, he wanted her to see them together. She pulled a face. Maybe it would teach her to keep a civil tongue in her head.

She changed her white wraparound

overall for a fresh one, checked her hair in the mirror and, taking a deep breath, picked up the tray and carried it into the magnificent dining-room. Tonight it wasn't a showroom in a stately home. It had been brought to life with the sparkle of crystal and silver and hothouse flowers, its vastness banished to the shadows by soft candlelight.

Two intimate figures were illuminated by the soft light. Jay, his hands holding the long fingers of Annabel Courtney, glanced up at her as she entered, in a manner calculated to irritate.

'Annabel wanted to meet my new cook, Kate.' There was a brazen possessiveness about the 'my' that set her teeth on edge. 'She was hoping you might be prepared to share your recipe.' The beautiful blonde sitting close to Jay, her fingers curved in his, would have turned any head: as the uncrowned queen of breakfast television it was like meeting someone you had known for years. But Kate was only conscious of Jay's eyes fixed upon hers as he lifted the woman's fingers to his lips. 'Or is it some closely guarded secret?'

Kate's hands tightened into small fists until the skin on her knuckles was bone-white. It was too blatant to miss. He intended her to see this. He was demonstrating his power in some way that she couldn't begin to understand. But if he had wanted to make her jealous he hadn't needed to go to so much trouble. While she had been alone in the kitchen, preparing each delicate little course, her imagination had been working overtime, doing his work for him.

She turned away from him, to face the woman who was eyeing her with undisguised interest. 'It's not a secret, Miss Courtney. You can have the recipe with pleasure. I'll demonstrate it on your breakfast programme whenever you like.'

Annabel's eyes widened and she glanced at Jay. 'Darling, what a brilliant

121

idea. Your own cook! Think of the publicity — '

'And . . . ' They both turned to look at Kate as she interrupted. 'And it has one other advantage. I'm certain that Miss Courtney will not expect the usual . . . privileges.' Annabel gasped and stifled something uncommonly like a giggle in her napkin.

Jay, however, was not in the least amused. 'That will be all, Kate,' he said abruptly, his voice frozen, his eyes like stone. She was dismissed like the servant she was.

Impetuously she bobbed a brief curtsy and, dropping her voice into the slow Norfolk dialect, she said, 'Yes, sir. Thank you, sir.'

'Kate!' She was halfway across the hall when his voice halted her. She turned slowly to face his wrath.

'What, sir?' she asked.

His breath came in a sharp hiss against his teeth. 'I won't be used,' he said, with razor-edged precision, glaring down his long nose at her.

She didn't have the advantage of his height, had to tilt her head to return his look, but he was left in no doubt as to her feelings. 'Neither will I, Mr Warwick. Not as an exhibit like a prize heifer at a show. And I think you owe Miss Courtney an apology too. Or maybe she's not as fussy.' She saw the spark of anger flash across his face and turned to go, satisfied to have touched him on the raw for once.

'Kate!' His command demanded instant respect and she paused, glad that her cheeks were still pink from the heat of the kitchen. 'One other thing.'

'What is it?'

'Don't ever curtsy to me again. Is that clear?'

'Yes, sir.' She dropped a quick bob, quite beyond seeing the danger. 'Is there anything else, sir?'

His arm shot out and he grabbed her, his face like thunder. 'I ought to put you over my knee and beat your backside. How dare you — '

'Jay, darling.' Annabel Courtney had

followed him to the door of the dining-room. 'I think perhaps I'd like to go home now.' She made the smallest gesture in their direction. 'Whenever you're ready, of course.'

For a moment Jay continued to stare at Kate, then he released her. 'Of course, Annie. We'll go now.'

Kate fled to the comparative safety of the kitchen. She was breathing a little more heavily than normal as she leaned against the door. But she knew he wouldn't follow her. He had Annabel Courtney to take his mind off his tiresome cook.

* * *

When the house closed at six on Sunday evening, Kate felt as if she had worked a shift as a stoker on a ship. By the time everything was cleared away she ached everywhere and all she wanted was a long soak in her bath and bed. Jay, however, would have none of it.

'You need some fresh air. Come on.'

She drew back as he threw his arm around her shoulders and ushered her towards the door. 'No, thank you.'

'You've hardly been out all week. You're so pale that I'll have the Royal Association for the Protection of Cooks after my blood. We'll take Daisy for a walk.'

She opened her mouth to repeat her refusal, then acquiesced without further protest. There was a determination about him that brooked no denial. And she knew he was right. If she fell into bed without winding down she would feel dreadful in the morning.

'I'll have to change.'

'Get a move on, then.'

She caught herself running up the stairs two at a time, and forced herself to a more sedate pace. It was ridiculous that her heart should be beating just that bit faster, she told her reflection, simply because he cared enough to see that she had 'some fresh air'. Last night all his care had been for Annabel Courtney.

She topped a pair of soft grey trousers, warm enough for a spring evening, with a toning silk shirt and pulled on her favourite deep rose sweater, but regarded her reflection with little satisfaction. She fluffed on a little blusher and touched her lips with colour. It had been a hard week but she knew her pallor had little to do with that.

Jay was waiting outside and he turned at the sound of her feet on the gravel. For a moment he was perfectly still. Then he moved to open the passenger door of the Range Rover for her.

'I thought we were going for a walk,' she said.

'We are.' He didn't elaborate and she scrambled up before he took it into his head to help her. It was an unnecessary precaution. He had already gone to the back of the Rover to lift Daisy in, then he climbed in beside her and headed north.

'Where are we going?' she asked, after a while.

'To the beach.'

'The beach?'

Her surprise made him laugh. 'I hope

you've no objection to getting sand in your shoes?'

'I can always take them off.'

'Why on earth did I stick at shoes?' he chided himself.

She ignored this remark. 'I hadn't realised we were so close to the sea.'

'Where did you think all those crabs come from?'

'The local fishmonger?' she asked, her expression one of total innocence.

He gave her a sidelong glance as they slowed for a flock of sheep to cross the road. 'Where else?'

Half an hour later they were following an ecstatic Daisy over the dunes. Kate laughed as the dog hurled herself after the seabirds with an enthusiasm undiminished by failure, as they rose effortlessly to avoid her and settled a few feet away.

'That's better. You should laugh more often.' Kate gasped as Jay caught her hand and set off running down the beach with her.

'Stop! Stop, Jay, please,' she begged

finally, sinking to the sand.

He threw himself down beside her, closer than was entirely comfortable, putting up a hand to stroke her cheek gently. 'Well, at least you've got some colour now.'

'Don't!' Kate exclaimed painfully, longing for him to touch her, yet dreading it, and she could see in his eyes that he knew. There was a dangerous moment. A moment of utter stillness when even the gulls seemed to hold their breath, and if he had reached for her she would have been lost. Then, quite deliberately, he rolled over on to his back and stared up at the darkening sky.

Kate sank back on to the sand and gradually her breathing returned to near normal. Something had happened and she didn't quite understand what it was. But the Jay Warwick she had met in Tisha's kitchen would not have turned away. He would have exploited the weakness he had seen in her eyes without a second thought for his victim.

Then Annabel Courtney's laughing

face filled her mind. Their names were often linked romantically. She had been Jay's companion for a long time. No matter how many other women he was seen with, she was always in the background. After last night it looked as if the romance was on again. And it hurt. She knew it shouldn't. Her desire was just the fevered response of urges woken from over long hibernation. She didn't even like the man, she reminded herself. But somehow that didn't quite ring true.

'I had another look at that video of the house today. You were really very good.' He turned his head towards her. 'I'm going to London tomorrow. I'll have one of the technicians make a copy for you. You should use it as an audition tape.'

She turned her head to look at him. 'What's an audition tape?'

'It's something to show television producers. Cuts out the need to work your way up through the beds of the lower orders.'

'Then thank you.' She scrambled to her feet and walked quickly away towards the sea, telling herself that it was the wind stinging tears to her eyes. She heard him coming up behind her and turned on him before he could say anything else to hurt her. 'Perhaps I'll try.' She sniffed. 'I would have liked a chance to do the breakfast show with Annabel, though.'

He caught her arms and held her. 'Get rid of Sam and I'll reconsider.'

'I had a letter from Sam today.'

'I noticed.'

'A thank-you note.' Ecstatic, full of dreams and joy to be doing what she wanted most in the whole world.

His mouth had become a thin hard line. 'And how much did he want this time?'

She allowed her eyes to drop. 'Not so much.' Just some money for new dancing shoes and tights and a leotard.

'Why on earth do you do it?' He shook her, but gently, as if he couldn't trust himself to show the true depth of his feelings. 'You're an idiot.'

'Am I?' Maybe she was an idiot. But not the kind he thought her. 'Maybe that is the difference between sex and love, Jay. Love makes us foolish, but you are far too clever to become ensnared. I feel almost sorry for you.'

5

His hands tightened on her shoulders and Kate felt a qualm of unease. 'Jay . . . I'm . . . '

'Sorry?' he asked, very softly.

She'd done it this time. How dared she presume to pity a man who had everything he could ever want? Power, wealth, and the most beautiful women in the world at the crook of his finger. Yet she didn't believe that Jay Warwick was a happy man, and for the first time she wondered what had happened that had made him so cynical about women.

'I shouldn't have said that, Jay. I'm sorry.'

The ominous glitter in his eyes disappeared as he considered this. 'An apology.' Suddenly the tension was gone as he laughed out loud. 'Now I'm *really* beginning to worry.' And taking her arm he led her back up the beach without another word.

In the distance the stark outline of a windmill was black against the pale evening sky and the seabirds were wheeling noisily as Daisy set them up. The sea was a long way off, but there was a sharp salty tang to the air that she could taste on her lips.

'We'll call at the pub on the way home. All that exercise has made me thirsty,' he said, as they shook the sand out of their shoes.

She didn't believe an answer was required. Instead she leaned against the Rover waiting for him to remove a large portion of the beach from Daisy, and stared up at the sky. 'It'll be dark soon.'

'Yes.' He frowned. 'You're not afraid of the dark, are you?' he asked, unlocking the door and helping her up.

'The dark? No, I love it here. It gets so much darker than in London. Really black. I never realised how many stars there were.'

'Millions. One for every grain of sand upon this beach,' he said.

'A philosopher,' she murmured as she fastened her seat-belt.

'No, a physicist. Or at least I should have been. Would have been if I hadn't filled in a couple of months helping out at a fringe festival in Edinburgh. I could have saved the taxpayer the cost of my education if I'd discovered my true vocation a little earlier.'

'Education is never wasted,' Kate said. 'Doubtless it comes in very handy for counting the money.'

He turned to her. 'That's better, Kate. I feel so much safer when you're being positively rude.'

She made her lips curve into a parody of a smile. But the sentiment was too similar to the way she felt about him. And that didn't make her feel safe at all.

A few minutes later he pulled up outside a tiny inn looking out over the marshes, and they went inside. He fetched two cold beers from the bar and for a while they sat together in the window-seat, watching the last colour fade from the sky and far out at sea the lights of passing ships.

'It was a good day, I think,' he said, at last. 'I wanted to say thank you for all your hard work.'

'I'm paid to do it. And I enjoyed the challenge.'

She was conscious of his arm along the back of the seat, brushing against her shoulders. She knew she should move. Not because she didn't want him to touch her, but because she wanted it too much and that was really idiotic. There was no future in touching Jay Warwick.

Jay's voice broke into her thoughts. 'You should wear your hair loose more often, Kate. It suits you.' He teased a long dark strand around his fingers.

'So I've been told.' She tried, too late, to move away, but he had her captive and was not about to let her go.

The small creases at the corners of his mouth deepened into a smile. 'Of that I have no doubt. Many times. So why do you hide it away? Don't you like to be told that you are beautiful?' She didn't answer. 'Or perhaps you only wear it loose for Sam? Does he take out the pins, one by one, until it tumbles about your shoulders? Does he brush it for you before he takes you to bed?'

The image he conjured up was too bewitching, too immediately seductive. She jerked away from him and gave a little yelp as she was brought up short by his firm grasp. 'Please, Jay!'

'You must be very beautiful lying against the pillows with it spread about you.'

'I'm not beautiful,' she protested. 'I'm just an ordinary girl, Jay. I live in the ordinary world. Why won't you leave me alone?'

'Confess, Kate.' She stared at him. He knew. He had been playing a game with her. Tisha must have told him, after all. 'Tell me the truth,' he insisted.

'I'm sorry.' She stared at her fingernails. 'I didn't mean . . . ' He waited. 'You've every right to be angry.'

'I'm not angry, Kate. Just say the

words. Confess that you'd forget all about Sam and how much you love him if I were to take you in my arms and make it my business to drive him out of your head?'

'What?' She had been going to aplogise for her deception, tell him the truth. But he was so determined on proving his own cynical point of view that he hadn't taken in what she had said.

'You're trembling, Kate. Are you afraid of me? Tell me,' he persisted softly. 'I'll do my best to help.'

'I don't need your kind of help,' she snapped, biting back tears too near the surface. 'And I'm not afraid of anything — '

'Nothing?' He raised his eyebrows dramatically. 'Everyone is afraid of something, even if it's only spiders in the bath.'

'Give me a call if you ever want one fished out,' she offered.

He regarded her steadily. 'Thank you. But with you in my bathroom I wouldn't notice a dozen spiders.' He smiled as a blush seared the fine bones of her cheeks. 'And it's your fears that we're discussing.'

'Short conversation, Jay.' Her irrational terror of thunder was a secret between her and Sam and she wasn't about to make a present of it to Jay Warwick. 'And I'm certainly not afraid of you. It's simply that I can see right through you and, frankly, I don't much like the view.'

'You are fooling yourself, lady, and I intend to prove it to you.' He spoke with utter conviction.

'Sam needs me, Jay,' she protested, desperately. 'You'll just have to take my word for it.'

'Of that I have no doubt. The point I'm trying to demonstrate is that you don't need him.'

'Surely that's for me to say?' She swallowed a yawn.

He hesitated for just a moment, then said, 'Come on. It's been a long day. I'll take you home.'

They travelled for twenty minutes or so in silence. There seemed nothing more to say, Kate thought, and as he drew up in the courtyard she gave him a brisk goodnight and before he could do or say anything to stop her she escaped and was safe inside the house.

She was sitting on the bed in her sensible striped pyjamas vigorously brushing her hair when she heard Jay's steps in the hall. She froze as they stopped outside her door.

'Goodnight, Kate,' he called, and laughed softly, as if he knew exactly the tremors he was causing in her breast. A moment later she heard his door close along the corridor and she flew to turn the key in the lock, hardly sure whether it was to keep Jay Warwick out, or herself in.

★ ★ ★

Wednesday was her day off and she spent the morning working on her column for the *Evening Mail*. She had hit on the idea while writing to Sam, dropping quite naturally into the chatty 'write-as-you-speak' style that she used for letters.

She had used a different 'voice', though. The well-remembered voice of an old lady who had told her endless stories of her life in service as a girl. The occupant of her 'country kitchen' was Cathy, a country girl who swopped recipes with her more sophisticated cousin Kate, who lived in London. In her first letter Cathy had described the house and Jack Wessex, a television personality who, she confided, had welcomed her very warmly when he had met her in the garden, asking Kate with disarming naïveté if it was the usual practice for employers to kiss the cook.

This week she was going to use a recipe for a vegetable terrine, enlivening it with a description of an heroic battle with an irascible gardener about which vegetables were ready to pull. But it needed a little more. A little bit of spice. Kate carried on typing.

I thought your comments about Mr Wessex were rather unkind, Kate. He says it's a well known fact that kissing the cook improves the sauce. I'm surprised that you didn't know that. And heaven knows, my sauces can do with all the help they can get . . .

Kate read it through, wondering if she had gone too far. Then she shrugged. No one would ever know it was Jay, and the editor would blue-pencil it quickly enough if she didn't like it.

'I'm going to the post, Tisha. Shall I take Daisy with me?' Kate put her head around the drawing-room door. Daisy didn't wait for a second invitation. Kate had a jacket on and that was good enough.

'Oh, thank you. Kate, I've been meaning to ask you. I play bridge at the vicarage on Wednesday evenings. It's rather dull, I know, but since you don't know anyone here yet I wondered if you would like to come along?'

'I'm afraid that I'm a total duffer at card games,' Kate apologised 'And Mike Howard invited me out tonight. Jay introduced us in Oulton Market the other day.'

Lady Maynard regarded her over the top of her spectacles with a suspicion of a smile. 'Then I hope you have a lovely time. Mike is a very pleasant young man.'

★ ★ ★

Lady Maynard was right. Mike was a pleasant companion. Easy to talk to and interesting on the subject of his work for the National Trust. Unthreatening. They had a meal in an old country house that had been converted to a restaurant.

'Thanks, Mike, for a lovely evening.' He had walked her across the courtyard to the door and they now stood a little uncertainly. Not intimate enough to kiss without the spark that made such an end to the evening inevitable, but something seemed to be required.

'Could we do this again soon, Kate?' Mike asked. 'I enjoyed myself enormously.'

Kate heard the earnestness in his voice with a touch of misgiving. She had enjoyed herself, but had no intention of encouraging Mike. Life was already complicated enough. A sudden flood of light illuminating them from the doorway put an end to all further conversation.

'Mike! How good of you to bring Kate home. Would you like to come in for a drink?' The words were right, but Jay's voice was not encouraging.

'Hello, Jay. I thought you were in London.'

'I was, but with so many attractions at Fullerton I find I just can't keep away.'

Mike looked uncomfortable. 'I'd better be off, Kate. I'll ring you later in the week.'

'Yes, do,' Kate called after him with a great deal more enthusiasm than she had felt two minutes earlier. Then she turned on Jay. 'Were you waiting behind the door?'

'Of course I was. I timed my entrance to perfection, don't you think? Another ten seconds and he would have kissed you.'

'And what if he had?' she demanded, angrily. 'What business is it of yours?'

'None. I was thinking of Sam,' he said, his grave concern a blatant mockery.

'Sam . . . ' Words failed her.

'You'd better come in.' He put a hand out and hauled her across the threshold. 'I do believe it's beginning to rain.'

Furious, she tried to push past him, but his fingers bit into her arm.

'Let go of me!' she demanded.

'Why? I'm sure that I can equal anything Mike Howard has to offer.' He hooked her into his arms with brazen ease and kicked the door shut.

Then, oblivious to her furious struggles, he kissed her with the unerring conviction that it was exactly what she wanted.

She didn't stop fighting him, furiously hammering at his shoulders and his arms. She knew if she did she would be utterly overcome by the urgent demand of his mouth on hers. But the potent force he exuded came close to overwhelming her. She felt her self-control slipping towards the edge and a desperate hungering need to take what he was offering and let the consequences go hang. She gave a final desperate push and then they were glaring at each other across a yard of kitchen, breathless and angry. She staggered, half falling on putty legs in her need to escape him. He moved to help her but she shook him off.

'Don't ever do that again!' The words tumbled from her.

'No one is going to kiss you on my doorstep, Kate,' he swore with absolute certainty. He towered over her, red-blooded, forceful. 'No one but me.' Each word was a hammer blow in her ears.

'Is that right?' She flinched under the onslaught. She wanted to run, but if she did not put a stop to this now it would get beyond her ability to control. He had taken no notice of her protestations of indifference, probably with good cause. But she had come too close to surrender tonight. Her eyes sparkled with fury that he could do this to her, and with the sharp sting of tears, and she retaliated. 'Well, let me tell you this, Jay Warwick. Lay one finger on me again and I'll lay a complaint against you for sexual harassment!'

The muscles of his neck stood out in cords as he fought to control himself, and it took every ounce of courage to stay there and stare him down. Not that he looked away. For endless paralysed moments they glared unblinking at each other.

'Jay?' It was as if the voice came from another planet. 'I didn't expect you until the weekend.'

So slowly that she could see the effort it took, Jay forced himself to relax and smile before turning to face his aunt. 'It's hot and dusty in London, Tisha. I've come in search of a little peace and quiet in which to work.'

'I think perhaps you carry the clamour around with you,' she said, drily. 'If you're planning to stay, I would be grateful if you could arrange for some secretarial help. When you're here the telephone never stops ringing. Did you have a pleasant evening, Kate?'

Kate blinked. She had forgotton Mike completely. 'Yes, thank you. How was the bridge?' she asked mechanically.

Lady Maynard removed her gloves, finger by finger, and regarded them both with a certain wry humour. 'I couldn't seem to concentrate and the vicar was furious with me. For a man of the cloth he is a very bad loser. Frankly, I could do with a drink. Kate? Will you join me?'

She shook her head. 'No, thank you. It's late and I've a long day ahead of me tomorrow.'

She moved quickly around Jay, avoiding a movement in her direction that she sensed rather than saw. She made no mistake about locking her door and lay stiffly, unable to sleep, unable even to think clearly, for a long time. She heard Lady Maynard walk along the corridor to her room, followed by the scuffling paws of Daisy, but hours later Jay had not passed her door and she wondered if he had turned around and driven straight back to London.

Finally, she decided to warm some milk and, pulling her dressing-gown tightly around her, she went downstairs.

A sound from the study stopped her as she crossed the hall and she froze, certain of burglars. A quiver of apprehension dried her throat, but she moved silently towards the half-open door. Jay was sitting in the dark. He had put a match to the fire, but it had long since died down and only the faintest glow illuminated the room and his outline slumped in the high-backed chair.

'Jay?' she said, uncertainly.

'What do you want?' His voice was discouraging.

'It's very late.'

'I can tell the time. What's the matter, Kate? Can't you sleep? Am I troubling your conscience?'

He had hit too close to the truth for comfort. As soon as her empty threat had left her lips she had wished it unsaid. Jay Warwick wasn't harassing her. It was her own body that was guilty of that.

'Would you like a warm drink? I thought I might make something? Cocoa, perhaps?'

'Cocoa! The last woman who offered me cocoa was my nanny!' he swung around and studied her in the light of the dying embers. 'She dressed rather like that, in striped pyjamas and a woolly dressing-gown. But they look rather different on you.' His eyes narrowed as he regarded her hair tumbled about her shoulders. 'And the hair. Perhaps you should invest in a hairnet and curlers if you plan to wander about the house at night half-dressed.' He turned back to the fire. 'Cocoa won't cure what ails me, Kate.'

'Then why don't you give Annabel a call?' she said, with a brave attempt at diversion.

'Annabel?' He raised a gallows smile. 'Annabel's in London, so you'd better go back to your bed. And be sure to lock your door.'

★　★　★

It was still raining when she finally gave up the strugle to sleep and climbed wearily out of bed. She pulled on an old tracksuit and set off for a run with Daisy, hardly noticing that her hair was plastered to her head and her tracksuit was sodden. Then she stood under a fierce shower to finish the job of waking up.

A sleepless night was no preparation for a hard day's cooking and every cherry, every date, every walnut seemed to have a life of its own as her fumbling fingers attempted to produce a series of perfect cakes.

She had not seen Jay. He had not

appeared for breakfast. Nancy had taken something through to the study on a tray and said that he wasn't to be disturbed. But his brooding presence filtered throughout the house, making everyone jumpy.

Tisha Maynard looked in briefly. 'I'm going to Norwich, Kate. I won't be back until late. Will you ask Nancy to leave me a sandwich in the pantry? I shan't need anything else and perhaps you could see to yourself. She normally has Thursday evenings off.'

'Of course. What about . . . ?' Her mouth dried on his name.

'Jay can go to the pub. It won't hurt him.'

'It's no bother.' Kate protested.

'Jay has a house and a staff of his own in London. If he wants to be waited on he should stay there.'

Nevertheless, when she decided to make a simple spaghetti bolognese for her supper there was more than enough for two.

She laid a place in the small

dining-room and then rang through from the kitchen to tell him what she had done, forcing a brisk, businesslike tone into her voice. Jay didn't answer for a moment.

'Thank you, Kate,' he said at last.

She put down the telephone and settled down to eat by herself, pushing the food around her plate, wondering why she had even bothered.

'Kate?' She jumped. Jay was standing beside her, his plate in one hand, a bottle of wine and two glasses in the other, and her heart gave an involuntary leap of pleasure. 'It seemed silly to sit in there on my own. Can I join you? Or will you throw something at me?' He hadn't slept. His cheeks were hollow and his eyes over-bright.

'Frankly, I'm not capable of throwing so much as a tantrum.'

He sat in the chair opposite her and poured two glasses of a dark red wine. He held a glass up, swirling it in the light. 'I brought this back from Tuscany last year. It's really rather good.'

He semed to be making an effort at normal conversation and Kate tasted the wine and agreed. They toyed with their food for a while in silence.

'Kate — '

'Jay — '

They both stopped. 'Don't go.' Jay's words fell into the silence.

'Go?'

'Isn't that what you're going to say? That you're leaving?'

'Leaving?' The word was shocking and she shook her head. 'No! I just wanted to say that I'm sorry about last night.'

'Sorry!' He was stunned. 'What on earth for?'

'You know why . . . '

'I was the one who behaved like a mindless oaf.' He stared at her. 'But when Tisha mentioned on the phone that you were going out with Mike I couldn't believe it. After all that high-minded stuff about how much you love Sam. How could you?' he demanded.

'It was just a pleasant evening out,

Jay. I'm quite capable of having a friendship with a man.'

'So next time *you* phone *him* and pick up the tab at the end of the evening?'

She knew he was right, but she persisted. 'Why not?'

'I doubt if Mike sees the relationship progressing in quite that way. He just isn't as frank about it as I am.'

She lowered her eyes. There was precious little frankness in their relationship. But she could put one thing right. 'Jay, I didn't mean what I said. About accusing you of . . . ' Kate broke off, unable to say the words. 'I wouldn't have done that.'

She felt him staring at her. 'You had every right.'

'Please, let's just forget it,' she begged, keeping her gaze firmly fixed upon her plate.

He reached across the table and lifted her chin with the tips of his fingers. 'Forget it? Just like that?' he asked, the faintest, self-mocking smile touching his eyes. 'You're very generous.'

Generous. The word mocked her. What would he say if he knew about the things she wrote in her column? she wondered. The wretched thing had taken on a life of its own. 'Cathy' had begun to receive mail from old ladies offering heartfelt advice to find a new employer as quickly as possible. Her editor had forwarded them and it was only by luck that she had been intercepted by the postman in the courtyard, happy not to have to get out of his van in rain, and been handed a manilla envelope with the *Evening Mail* logo printed large in the corner along with the rest of the post. Tense as a bow-string, she gave up any pretence of eating.

After a while Jay said, 'Kate, I've been approached by a children's charity who want to hold a Teddy Bear's Picnic in the grounds. What do you think?'

She made an effort, dragged her mind back from its misery. 'It would be good publicity. I'm sure you'd get plenty of coverage in the press.'

'That would be an added bonus, but it is a cause I happen to hold rather dear.'

A children's charity? Shaken she said, 'I'm sorry. I didn't mean to be flippant. I think it's a great idea.'

'I'd like to open the Conservatory for them. Since we'd have to do it on a Saturday and the house will be open again on the Sunday it will mean a great deal of extra work. Can you manage that?' He sat forward, pushing the plates to one side.

She saw with some surprise that it really was important to him. 'Of course we can manage. Have you a date in mind?'

'Towards the end of May. I have the letter in the study. I'll get my office to go ahead and organise some advance publicity.' He offered her another glass of wine. Kate shook her head, stifling a yawn. 'Perhaps you're right. Besides, I have to walk that dratted dog.' He rose. 'Will you come with me? It's stopped raining.'

'I don't think — '

'I'll make you a promise, Kate.' He took her hands and drew her to her feet. 'The next time I kiss you it will be at your invitation.' He placed a finger on her lips before she could protest. 'And I would be grateful for the company. I've been holed up in the study all day, working on some figures. Penance enough, believe me. Besides, I've a couple of other ideas I'd like your opinion on.' He was still holding her hand as he opened the door.

* * *

Jay arrived from London one Friday evening with a package. She was working in her tiny office and looked up as his shadow fell across her desk.

'This is yours, Kate.' He took a videotape from the envelope. She had forgotten all about it and for a moment couldn't think what it was. 'It's you doing your stuff for the television. Sorry it's taken so long.'

157

'Thank you.' She looked at the newspaper clippings he was holding and a quiver of alarm shot through her. 'What are those?'

'The press cutting agency I use sent all the Fullerton Hall clippings to me in London. I thought you might like to see them.'

She let out a careful breath. 'I can't believe there are so many.'

'They're not all the result of the publicity. Some just mention the house.' He flipped through them. 'This one might amuse you.' She took the slip of newsprint he offered.

''Where is Kate?'' she read and looked at him.

'What is this?' He merely smiled and she read on. ''Fun-loving bachelor Jay Warwick has been keeping his head down lately, apparently far too busy with the opening of his stately home in Norfolk to frequent his usual nightspots. Of course, it might just be the mysterious Kate who's keeping him so busy . . . '' Her voice trailed away.

'What on earth does that mean?'

'I'm afraid I took your name in vain one night on the television.' Kate remembered only too well the numbing shock. 'Very silly of me under the circumstances. Am I forgiven?' he asked carelessly.

'It was nothing. Really,' she said quickly.

'Ah, so you saw the programme?' His eyes sparkled. 'You never told me.'

'Sam had it on,' she said, without thinking, and the light died from his eyes. 'I wasn't watching particularly,' she lied. 'If you'll excuse me I have to get on with dinner.'

'Please don't cook for me. I'm eating out tonight,' Jay said.

'I noticed Annabel Courtney was home again. It must be very convenient having her so close.'

'Very.'

* * *

Mike telephoned after dinner to ask her if she could spare the time for a drink

159

and she forced herself to go out. Anything was better than sitting alone wondering what Jay and Annabel were doing. The thought induced a spasm of guilt, and when Mike brought her home she allowed him to kiss her. There was none of the helter-skelter of emotion she had experienced when Jay kissed her, but Mike didn't seem to notice anything lacking.

'Dinner next week?' he asked.

Headlights in the drive panicked her. 'Ring me, Mike.' She fled indoors, anxious to get up to her room. But Daisy whined to go out, and she was still struggling into her outdoor shoes when Jay walked in. Her fingers were lifeless as she fought with the laces and he bent and tied them firmly for her. When he looked up, his face was inches from her own.

'Pleasant evening, Kate?'

'Yes,' she said, her heart ragged in her throat. 'Thank you.'

'No need to thank me. I'm sure you thanked Mike very adequately.' He stood up and walked quickly away.

'Damn!' Daisy nuzzled against her cheek, and Kate rubbed her head. 'Come on, girl. Let's go.'

★ ★ ★

Life proceeded peacefully enough. Jay came and went without warning, courteous but distant. If Kate's heart lifted disquietingly at each appearance, she coped. At least he made no further raids on her emotions. He was too occupied with Annabel, as their picture in the gossip columns constantly reminded her.

She continued to write her column for the *Evening Mail*, adding little snippets gleaned from her day-to-day work, hard pushed to fulfil her editor's demands to hear more of Jack and his wicked ways. Since their clash over Mike, Jay had been on his best behaviour and there had been little to write.

She heard nothing more of Mike. She

was somewhat surprised and slightly relieved, but on a mission to buy stamps in the post office in Oulton Mrket she saw him come in and waved. He abruptly turned and walked out. For a moment Kate could hardly believe it had happened. Then she abandoned her place in the queue and went after him.

'Mike!'

Cornered in the marketplace, he could do nothing else but stop and face her.

'Oh, Kate,' he said unenthusiastically. 'Hello.'

'How are you?' she asked, with a determined smile. 'I haven't heard from you lately.'

'I've been a bit busy.' She had the feeling that he was trying to avoid her eye and he glanced at his watch as if in a tremendous hurry.

'Me too. And the queue in the post office was terribly long. I'll go back later.' He looked distinctly uncomfortable and a nagging suspicion drove her on. They were outside the Black Lion. 'How about a drink?' she offered. 'It's my turn to buy you one.'

Mike looked at his watch again. 'I'd love to, Kate. But really I have to get on. I have an appointment.'

'Do you, Mike? Really?' She made no move to release him. She wanted to know what was going on. 'Or are you just trying to avoid me?'

He opened his mouth to protest, then he shrugged. 'I'm sorry, Kate, but Jay told me — '

'Jay!' she interrupted. 'What has he got to do with anything?'

He finally looked her straight in the face. 'He warned me off.'

She felt the colour drain from her face. 'Warned you off?' Her voice was faint. She hadn't known exactly what she expected but it was hardly that.

'*Droit de seigneur* and all that.' Mike's face was dark with embarrassment. 'You should have told me, Kate.' He turned and walked quickly away.

'Should I?' she whispered, staring at the envelope in her hands. 'Of course I should. Why not tell everyone?'

6

Kate ripped the envelope to shreds and dropped the pieces into a nearby litter bin. Tame stuff. Her editor said her readers wanted to hear more details of Cathy's life in the country. Well, she would give it to them. But she didn't honestly think they would believe it.

Her fingers flew over her typewriter keys as if possessed, and when at last she sat back and quickly read through what she had written, she gave a little gasp, hardly able to believe the words had come from her. But it was all true, she told herself as she stuffed the sheets into an envelope, and she posted it before she could change her mind.

Yet even as the envelope dropped from her fingers and was beyond recall she felt a tremor of apprehension. She had been able to justify her private joke because no one would ever know it was

Jay. But she knew that this time it had gone far beyond a joke and as she stood there, her fingers curled around the opening of the letterbox, she remembered the newspaper clipping that Jay had shown her. If her editor had seen it she could hardly fail to make the connection.

She turned and walked slowly back to the house. Her column had been an escape valve, relieving the steam vent of blind rage when she realised what Jay had done. It had worked, but as she turned away from the postbox she knew that she could never do it again. 'Cathy' would be taking the good advice of her anxious correspondents and leaving her employment with Jack Wessex. Her eyes sparked. It would serve him right if cousin Kate took over . . .

★ ★ ★

She didn't see Jay until the weekend and she was so busy that it was easy to keep out of his way. But Sunday evening after dinner he cornered her in her office.

'I've hardly seen you all weekend, Kate,' he said, coming up when she was deep in concentration on her accounts.

'There's been a lot to do,' she countered, and carried on determinedly, although all the figures had quite suddenly scrambled in her brain and her studious application was pretence.

'I want to settle the final details of the charity picnic. Let's walk down to the pub and discuss it over a drink.'

'I'd rather do it here.' She shifted a pile of papers from the only other chair in the little room.

He ignored this invitation and lodged himself alongside her on the edge of the table. 'So. You are deliberately avoiding me. I wasn't absolutely sure.' She didn't trust herself to reply. 'Why?' he demanded, clearly angered by her silence. 'I thought we'd decided upon a cease-fire. I can't recall anything that I've done recently to offend you.'

'Can't you? Perhaps you should think a little harder.' Her voice was tight and she swallowed in an attempt to ease her throat. He was too close, leaning over her, one hand on the back of her chair trapping her there.

'Why don't you just tell me, Kate?'

She ignored this. 'I'm ready to discuss work with you, Jay, nothing else.' She forced herself to look up into his face, confront the slight frown that creased his brow. She could almost have believed he had no idea what she was talking about. 'You did say that you wanted to talk about the arrangements for the picnic?'

For a long moment he stared at her. Then he pushed himself upright. 'In my study in ten minutes.' He turned on his heel and was gone.

She felt like the condemned man watching the clock creep around to the hour of execution. In the end it was almost a relief to rise and walk to the study door. She tapped.

'Come in!' His voice was impatient.

He was sitting at his desk, his attention entirely devoted to a sheet of paper before him. 'Why the formality, Kate? You don't bother to knock when you wander about in your dressing-gown.' He spoke without lifting his head and she didn't answer, but lowered herself on to the chair in front of his desk.

His voice clipped, he went through the details of the charity event: publicity, the celebrities who had promised to put in an appearance, among them Annabel Courtney. His businesslike manner steadied her pulse and for a while they worked coldly and efficiently.

Finally he threw down his pen and took off his glasses. 'Everything is apparently under control. Thanks, you've been a great help.'

'I'm sure that it will be a great success,' she said.

'All we need is a dry day and I've put in a special order with my weatherman.'

'In that case, nothing can go wrong.' She stood up and turned to go.

'Kate, that was a joke,' he said, with a

touch of irony. 'Either get whatever's bothering you off your chest or lighten up.'

Kate felt the colour rising to her cheeks but she had brought this confrontation on herself. 'I saw Mike in Oulton Market,' she said, hoping that would be sufficient to put an end to the subject.

'How nice for you both,' Jay said, and the cyncial twist to his mouth stirred the damped-down embers of her anger.

'No, as it happens. Embarrassing is the word that springs most readily to mind.'

'Really? Whatever could he have said that might embarrass you?' he asked, apparently finding the idea that Mike could embarrass anyone quite remarkable. 'I thought your relationship was supposed to be platonic?'

'He said . . . ' She found she couldn't repeat what he had said.

'Yes?' She had the uncomfortable sensation that he was playing with her and she didn't like it.

'You know exactly what he said,' she snapped.

'He told you about our little chat?'

'Little chat?' she finally exploded. 'Is that how you would describe it? How dare you discuss me as if I were ... ?' She was too outraged to go on. He hadn't even bothered to deny it.

'I know what I said, Kate, but I cannot begin to guess what he said to get you in such a state.' He shrugged and walked across to the side table and poured himself a brandy. 'Would you like one?' She shook her head, too vexed by his high-handed behaviour to speak. Jay sipped his drink thoughtfully. 'I had Sam in mind, you see.'

Her head came up involuntarily. 'What about Sam?'

'Have you forgotten how much you love him?' One dark brow kicked up in question. Kate's mind went blank, but he was clearly waiting for her to say something. Justify her apparent perfidy.

'Sam knows that ... he will always come first.'

'Does he? I find his faith in you quite touching.' He swallowed the brandy and regarded her with glittering eyes. 'Then perhaps we should consider Mike's feelings. I've known him a long time. I wouldn't want him to be hurt.'

She felt the colour drain from her cheeks. 'Your loyalty to your friends is commendable, Jay.' If she didn't know better. 'But I think perhaps he misunderstood your meaning. Maybe you weren't very clear in your choice of words.'

He shrugged. 'I didn't spell it out in words of one syllable. Mike's a bit of a prude, as I'm sure you've already noticed.'

Stung, she attacked. 'If by prudish you mean he doesn't proposition defenceless women going about their legitimate business, I'm inclined to agree with you.'

'Well, that makes a change in itself.' He poured himself another drink and without asking passed one to her. 'Although I think *defenceless* rather overstates your case. You seem eminently capable of defending yourself.' He regarded her steadily. 'You do it so well, in fact, that one might be inclined to wonder why you find it necessary?'

She nervously sipped the brandy, choking as the spirit caught the back of her throat. When he had finished thumping her back they were standing together and his arm was around her.

'Try again.' He offered her the glass. 'And this time take your time.'

'No!' She drew back from the glass and he put it down, but his arm remained about her shoulder and he tilted her face up, regarding it dispassionately.

'You're looking tired, Kate. You're doing too much. I'll organise some more help for you.'

'There's no need,' she said stiffly, and raced on, trying to ignore the warm touch of his fingers against her skin. 'It's a lot easier than working freelance in London. No late nights.'

For a moment his eyes darkened,

then he said, 'Perhaps that's the problem. You're not getting out enough. And the solution is simplicity itself. I've a couple of tickets to the theatre next week in Norwich. We'll have dinner afterwards.'

She felt near to hysteria. What girl in her right mind would turn him down? But then she hadn't been in her right mind since she had met the man. 'Couldn't Annabel spare the time?' she asked, provoked by the almost mindless response of her body to the touch of his fingers against her skin.

'Annabel . . . ' The name snapped from his lips and for a moment she thought she had gone too far. Then he released her and turned away, so that she could no longer see his eyes. 'No, Annabel can't spare the time. She's working this week.' He turned back to her, the cool, cynical expression firmly back in place. 'And since I've apparently robbed you of your beau — ' he paused ' — unless of course you've made it up with Mike?' She glared at

173

him. 'No?' He poured himself another drink. 'If it's so difficult to accept a simple invitation, Kate, I can always make it an order.'

'No, Jay. There's no need for that.' The situation between them had deteriorated far enough. She had already exacted revenge in her own way. They had to work together, and it was hardly his fault that she was quite unable to keep tight hold on her emotions when he was within twenty yards. 'I'll be happy to go with you.'

★　★　★

They arrived late at the theatre but, far from drawing censure, they were shown to their seats by the front of house manager just as the lights went down.

The play was *Noises Off*, a furiously paced comedy set backstage in a theatre, and within minutes they were both laughing furiously. By the interval Kate had quite forgotten that she had ever been angry with Jay.

They bypassed the crush bar. Instead Jay led the way backstage to the green room, introducing her simply as Miss Thornley to several formally dressed couples, who clearly knew him well and went out of their way to make her feel welcome.

Kate was glad she had taken so much trouble with her appearance. She only had one 'best' dress, made for a Christmas party. But the glowing burgundy silk was the perfect foil for her fair skin and had the classic good looks that would take it anywhere. She had left her hair loose and it hung, straight as a yard of tap water, black and shining down her back. As a final touch she fastened the ruby studs that her father had given her for her eighteenth birthday in her ears and nervously surveyed her reflection. She might have been pressganged into this evening out with Jay, but she was determined not to look like second-best.

He had been standing in the hall,

his back to the stairs, talking on the telephone as she'd walked down the wide oak staircase earlier this evening, feeling rather like a film star in an old movie. Except that all the glamour was Jay's. He had looked so different in formal clothes. His hair, dark, firmly under control for once, was touched by the rays of the evening sun slanting through the side windows. The black cloth of his dinner-jacket clung to his shoulders, emphasising their broad power. She'd been unaware of the little sigh that escaped her lips.

He had turned as he heard her, replaced the receiver and watched for a moment as she'd made her way down the stairs. Then he had moved swiftly across the hall and grasped her hands as she drew level with him. She paused a step above him and smiled up at him, suddenly shy.

'Cinderella, as I live and breathe.'

Kate's already flushed cheeks had grown pinker. 'Just make sure I'm home by midnight, Prince Charming,' she'd warned, to cover her confusion at his unexpected admiration.

'Don't tell me this turns into one of those unglamorous aprons you delight in?' Before she could answer he'd laughed. 'No. I have it. Not an apron. The dreaded striped pyjamas!'

He hadn't expected a response, for which she'd been grateful, instead ushering her through the front door and over the stone bridge to a black limousine. The chauffeur had opened the door and Jay had handed her in, settling down beside her.

'This is very grand, Jay.'

'Do you think so?'

She had felt stupid and naïve. Annabel Courtney would never have said anything so crass. As if he realised, he had taken her hand and raised it to his lips. 'I'm glad you like it.' And he'd tucked her hand under his arm and kept her amused all the way to the theatre, with stories about the celebrities she had seen on the television.

* * *

By the time they left the theatre Kate was aching with laughter. The car was waiting for them at the rear of the theatre away from the noisy, milling crush of people at the entrance.

'I really enjoyed myself. Thank you,' she said, as he slid in beside her.

'I noticed,' he said, and Kate felt her cheeks grow warm, glad of the darkness to cover her blushes. 'I like a woman who's not afraid to laugh.'

'Is that a compliment?' she asked impetuously.

'Aren't you sure?' He moved closer and took her hand in his. 'I'll clearly have to try a little harder.'

'That's not necessary,' she said quickly, and regained possession of her fingers. 'Where are we going?'

'A little restaurant quite near Oulton Market. It used to be a water-mill.'

The mill was delightful, built across a fast-flowing stream, and they had to walk across a small wooden bridge to reach the dining-room, where they were immediately shown to a table by the window. Kate looked out across the stream. Floodlights lit the exterior and the ducks sleeping on the grass. 'This is lovely, Jay.'

'I was sure you would like it.' A waiter appeared to serve them food. 'I knew we would be late so I ordered earlier this evening. I hope you don't mind?'

'You've taken a lot of trouble.'

'The greater the effort, the sweeter the reward.'

Her heart gave a little flip. 'And what reward are you seeking?'

'A smile will do, Kate. For now.'

For now. And afterwards? Was he so confident of his power to lure her into his bed? The trouble was that, although her heart had been deep-frozen since she had broken with David, this infuriating man had managed somehow to melt that protective layer.

She was staring at her theatre programme and now, through all this

179

confused thought, the Magnum logo jumped out at her from the inside cover.

'You sponsored the play,' she said, and avoided giving him the smile that she knew would have indicated her surrender. She looked up at him and for just a moment she caught a spark of something dangerous flash in his eyes. Then he leaned back in his chair and the moment passed.

'Not personally, Kate. Magnum takes an interest in provincial theatre.'

'That's why you were bowed all the way to your seat, despite being so late.'

'We were *both* bowed all the way to our seats, Kate,' he said, a little sharply. 'I did warn the front-of-house manager in advance. We arrived late because I preferred not to embarrass you by subjecting you to the speculation of gossip.'

'You're not normally so retiring.' She caught her lip between her teeth, as if trying to prevent the words from escaping, but too late. It was always too late. She couldn't seem to help it.

He smiled a little grimly. 'When I take a model or a hopeful young actress to a London club, she will expect to see her picture in the newspaper the next day. It's part of the deal.' For a moment his face chilled. 'We both know exactly what's expected of us.'

'I see.'

'No, Kate. I very much doubt it.' And for a moment his eyes remained like stone. Then he glanced at her and his mouth straightened in a smile. 'You, however, are as unexpected as the sun on a bank holiday. Definitely not for the gossip columns.' A cold hand touched her spine and she shivered as her mind jerked to the copy already lying on her editor's desk for the following week's column.

'Is there anything else? Or shall we eat?'

'I'm sorry. It's none of my business.' She picked up a fork. 'But it was a special occasion. That was why those people were in the green room to meet you? Why did you take me?'

His smile was touched with exasperation. 'I took you because I wanted to, Kate. Is there anything else?'

'But suppose I'd mentioned that I was your cook?' She was suddenly horror-struck at the thought.

He seemed to find the idea amusing. 'They would have taken one look at you and assumed you were using a euphemism for something rather different.'

She gave a little gasp. 'They wouldn't!' But even as she said it she knew he was right, and blushed.

'But since you are my cook, dear Kate, perhaps you would give me your professional opinion on this.'

The food was wonderful. A simple salad of baby lettuce, anchovies and croutons, followed by poussin which they ate with their fingers.

'Well?' He regarded her with amusement.

'It was quite wonderful.'

'There's more.'

'No. Not another thing. I couldn't.'

Then she sighed as a large bowl of fresh strawberries was placed on the table.

'What was that you were saying?'

'Nothing,' she said weakly. During the course of the meal he had gradually drawn from her her plans to open a restaurant of her own. Now, as they dipped the berries into sugar and cream, he said, 'This is the secret, you know. Simple food. None of that art-on-a-plate nonsense. I hope you're not going to indulge in that.'

'I'd like somewhere just like this some day.'

'And in the meantime?'

'For now I'd settle for anything I can afford.'

'Does it have to be in London?'

She nodded. 'Yes. Or somewhere near.' She would have to be close to Sam. She wouldn't have the time to travel long distances.

'Well, when are you going to do it?'

She sighed. 'When I have enough money. And you have to have something special to draw people to you.

Now when I've published my cookery book . . . ' she joked.

'A book?' He was immediately interested. 'How far have you got?'

'It's still at the idea stage, but basically I plan to adapt it from my cookery column in the *Evening* . . . ' slow colour burned her cheeks as she realised what would be in her column this week ' . . . in my local newspaper,' she went on. He might just be interested enough to look for himself if he knew she wrote for one of the London evening papers.

'Well, I wish you luck. But I think we'd better move,' Jay said.

Kate looked around and was surprised to see the restaurant was empty. 'It's late.'

'Well past midnight, Cinderella. Come along.'

The car purred to a halt in front of the hall and Jay walked her over the bridge, with its stone lions standing guard, and unlocked the front door.

He turned to her and, gently lifting

her chin, raised her face to his. 'Thank you for this evening, Kate. I hope you enjoyed yourself as much as I did.'

Suddenly shy at the warmth in his eyes, her heart beating up in her throat, Kate smiled up at him. 'I had a lovely time. Thank you, Jay.' Relaxed, happy, she knew that when he kissed her it would make the evening quite perfect. She closed her eyes in expectation of his embrace.

'If you want me to kiss you, Kate, you'll have to ask me.' Her eyes flew open. 'We had a deal, remember?'

Oh, lord, she wanted him to kiss her. It was unbearable; *he* was unbearable!

He laughed. 'I'll see you on Saturday.' He was halfway to the car before she realised that he was going.

'Jay?' He looked back at her, his hair touched with silver in the moonlight.

'Too late, sweetheart. I have to be in London at six. An interview with the Home Secretary. I'll only just make it.'

Leaning against the door, she watched until the car had quite disappeared beyond the church. Then slowly she turned and went inside. She should be furious with him, but she couldn't be. She had no one but herself to blame. He had been kind tonight. Kinder than she deserved. He had taken her out and given her a pleasant evening. But she had made the ground rules and it was ridiculous to be upset because for once he had decided to stick to them.

★ ★ ★

The weather held. Saturday was a brilliant day and they hoped for a big turn-out. There had been a spot about the picnic on local radio and, because so many celebrities had promised to support the event, the regional television people were expected to put in an appearance as well.

Kate had been glad of the extra work to keep her mind off Jay and what might have happened if he had kissed her. And there was the added worry about Sam's imminent arrival. She wasn't going to fetch her until Monday, when Jay would be safely away in the United States, but even so, it seemed unlikely that she would be able to keep up the pretence for much longer. She would have to tell him. This weekend.

'Hi, Kate! I thought I'd find you in the kitchen.'

She spun around, and a surge of pleasure at the sight of her sister carried her across the room. Pleasure that was immediately replaced by panic.

'Sam! What on earth are you doing here?' Horrified, she looked at her watch. She grabbed the girl as she heard Jay's voice in the hall and pushed her up the back stairs and along the corridor into her bedroom. 'I was coming to fetch you on Monday!'

'I know. But it was brilliant. One of the teachers was coming this way for half-term so I had a lift . . . '

'You can tell me later. Right now I'm thinking.' Sam wasn't the sort of girl to stay shut up on a day like this. 'Wretch,' she moaned. 'Why on earth did you have to turn up now?'

'That's not very nice. I thought you would be pleased . . . ' Sam complained, but Kate didn't have time to listen.

'You'll just have to get lost in the crowds until I've had a chance to explain to Jay.'

'This is some welcome,' Sam grumbled. Then she stopped, seeing that it was useless to protest.

'You should have thought of that before accepting lifts.' She frowned. 'Who gave you a lift anyway?' She went pale. 'You didn't hitch, did you?'

'I *told* you . . . '

'There isn't time now.' She opened the door a crack to check that the coast was clear before hurrying Sam down and out of the front door, where she stood uncertainly for a moment.

Another thought struck her. 'Have you got any money?' She sighed. It had been a silly question. She pushed a five-pound note into her hand. 'Off you go. Keep your head down and don't get into any trouble.'

'Anyone would think I was a criminal or something.'

'Or something,' she said, without hesitation. She watched as Sam wandered off and joined the growing crowds streaming into the park.

'Oh, lord,' she said to herself.

'Kate? Everything all right?' Jay appeared from the shadows and she gave a nervous start as he moved forward. 'You positively jumped. What's up? Is your conscience troubling you?' He laughed at her stricken expression and took her hand, then frowned. 'You're trembling. What's the matter?'

'Nothing.' And it was true that the trembling had nothing to do with Sam's unexpected arrival. It was the first time she had seen him since he had taken her out and she had spent those days dwelling on thoughts of what might have been. Even though he would only have wanted a brief affair, given a second chance she knew it was a risk she would be prepared to take. At least they would both know what they were

189

getting into. She tucked an escaped strand of hair behind her ear and pulled away. 'It's been a bit hectic, that's all.'

'Well, let's sit down for a few minutes before the rush begins.' He put his arm in hers and led her back to the kitchen. 'I'm sorry to be so late. I had to make a diversion to pick up one of our guests.'

'Have you had lunch? I could make you an omelette. It wouldn't take a minute.' There was a shake to her voice and a tendency to babble. Calm down, Kate, she told herself firmly.

'I've had lunch. Who was that girl I saw you talking to? She looked familiar somehow.'

Kate blenched. 'I need to talk to you, Jay,' she said, quickly. 'I have to explain something — '

'Darling! This is where you're hiding.' Annabel Courtney glanced around. 'What a lovely kitchen. And Kate, too. Thank you so much for sending me your recipe.' She came forward, hand outstretched. 'I do wish you could come on the programme to show us all how to do it. Even better, we could film it here,' she said, looking around. 'It would be perfect. Jason?' She smiled up him, with winning blue eyes. 'Darling, please say yes.'

'Forget it, Annabel,' he instructed.

Kate took the proffered hand and managed a smile to cover the sickening clutch of jealousy that seized her. Jay said he had given someone a lift. She should have realised it was Annabel. No wonder the diversion had taken so long. The woman, unaware of the bewildering ferocity of the emotion she had provoked in Kate, leaned forward and murmured confidentially, 'I'm afraid Jay doesn't like his girls running off to appear on the television.' She ignored the warning hiss that escaped Jay's lips. 'He prefers to keep them tucked up at home.'

'In bed?' Kate replied, the shocking words out of her mouth before she was even aware she had thought them.

7

Annabel's blue eyes flickered between them, speculation adding an extra lustre. 'Jay, my darling, whatever have you been doing to this young woman to give her such an impression of you?' She shook her head and tutted. 'If you're not very careful you'll be getting yourself a reputation.' She chuckled, delighted with her joke, then possessively linked her arm in his. 'Come along, I have to cut a ribbon, or declare something open, don't I?'

'This isn't a supermarket, Annie,' he said irritably as they left the kitchen, but he paused briefly in the doorway and turned to look back at Kate, a slight frown creasing his brow.

★　★　★

There had been a steady trickle of grandparents to the Conservatory all afternoon, but they hadn't been rushed and Kate had allowed the girls to go out for a while in turn to join in the fun. But towards the end of the afternoon they began to get very busy and Kate found herself carrying trays through to the waiting customers.

'I saw you on the telly, dear,' one woman was saying. 'I said to my sister . . . ' But Kate wasn't listening. Her sharp ears had caught the brief swirl of an ambulance siren, and a shout, and she looked out of the window across to the lake where a small crowd was beginning to gather and more people were hurrying across the park to see what had caused the fuss. She moved to the door. 'What's happened?' she asked one of the estate workers.

'Someone's fallen into the lake,' he said. 'I'm just going to call the doctor.'

'Who?' she demanded.

'No one local,' he called back. 'A young girl, that's all I know.'

Kate began to walk across the grass, numbly at first, one foot in front of another, with a sudden sickening premonition of disaster. Then she began to run.

She came to an abrupt halt at the sight by the lakeside. A St John Ambulance nurse had wrapped Sam in a blanket and she was sitting inside the ambulance, shivering, her long hair dripping about her shoulders, her teeth chattering. 'S . . . sorry, Kate. I did try not to get into any trouble, but a little boy's teddy fell in the lake . . . Are you very cross with me?'

Relief that she was apparently all right turned Kate's anguish to anger. 'A teddy bear! You risked your life for a teddy bear! Samantha Thornley, have you any idea how *dangerous* that lake is?' Tisha Maynard had warned her how steeply it shelved. She glanced at the ambulanceman. 'Is she going to be all right?'

'She'll be fine. A hot bath should do it,' he said, reassuringly. 'She's just got a soaking. Mr Warwick insisted on sending for the doctor, but . . . ' The man smiled at someone behind her. 'The young lady will be quite all right, sir . . . '

Kate spun around and confronted the author of this disaster, shock blinding her to everything but the fact that her sister could have drowned. 'This is all your fault,' she said bitterly. 'There should have been warnings, someone here to stop this happening. Children can't help falling into water . . . '

'I'm not a child,' Sam protested vehemently.

Kate turned on her. 'Then why were you acting like one?'

'Kate, for heaven's sake, she was just trying to help — ' Jay protested.

'Help! And where were you when all this was happening?'

'I was here,' he said, a little grimly.

'You! And I suppose you're a trained life-saver? She could have drowned.'

'Kate, I can swim,' Sam objected. 'I just lost my footing. I didn't expect it to be so slippery . . . '

'Why should you? There were no

notices . . . no warning signs . . . ' She suddenly became aware of the large number of people gathered around, staring in open fascination as she berated Jason Warwick. 'Come on. The doctor's coming and we'd better get you out of these wet things.' She helped her down the step, pointedly ignoring Jay, but Sam stopped.

'Thank you for pulling me out of the lake, Mr Warwick.' She grinned, clearly over the worst. 'Just wait until the girls at school hear about it. It was quite worth the soaking . . . '

He smiled at the girl. 'I'm glad you think so. But please promise me you won't do anything like it again.' Kate suddenly realised that Jay's shoes and trousers were wet and thickly coated in mud.

'I promise.'

'Is the young lady all right?' a young woman interrupted anxiously. She was holding a boy, about two years old, his cheeks streaked with dirt where the tears had run. Now he was simply staring wide-eyed at Sam, clutching a soaking wet bear.

'I'm fine,' Sam said. 'I'm glad you've got your bear back.' A flurry of flashes announced the arrival of the press and several reporters gathered around them.

Jay grabbed Kate by the arm. 'Let's get out of here,' he said.

'But I can't leave Sam . . . '

'Sam?' Nothing had outwardly changed, yet she saw the spark of something dangerous deep in his eyes. And she shuddered. She had wanted to pick her moment to tell him, but she had left it too late. And now he was angry.

'My sister,' she said. He waited. 'Samantha. Everyone calls her Sam.'

He glanced at the slender, laughing girl, the centre of attention of a small crowd that had gathered around her, her hair already drying out in the sunshine. 'That is *Sam*?'

'I tried to tell you once.'

'Really? And when was that, Kate?' he demanded, a small muscle working at the corner of his mouth. 'When you were telling me how much you loved *him*? Or how you had to support *him*? Or the numerous other occasions that *he* came into the conversation?'

'I didn't start it. You leapt to the wrong conclusion!' she declared.

'And you didn't bother to enlighten me. I wonder why?'

For a moment the two of them stood locked together in a silent battle, his fingers biting deeper into her arm.

A sudden flash interrupted them. 'Thanks, Mr Warwick.' A grinning photographer waved his camera. 'What's your name, dear?'

'None of your damned business,' Jay retorted. He turned and hurried with her towards the house. 'Your sister isn't the only one who'll be appearing in tomorrow's papers.'

'It doesn't matter,' she said crossly, looking back across her shoulder. 'Sam!'

Jay pushed her through the door. 'It does to me.'

Of course it did. Annabel had been the girl on his arm in the gossip columns recently.

'I'm sorry if it will embarrass you,' she said stiffly. She raised her chin, unaware that her wide grey eyes were sparkling with unshed tears.

'Oh, God! Nancy! Hot sweet tea, quick as you can. In the study, it'll be quiet in there. I've got to get into some dry clothes.'

She protested. 'I have to look after Sam! She'll get pneumonia.'

'In this heat? I don't think so. But she might just pass out from the smell of this mud.'

'You've had a shock, Kate. Come along,' Nancy insisted, with a stubbornness that would not be moved. 'I'll take care of your sister, but you've had a shock yourself.' She was adamant that Kate put her feet up on the sofa by the window, promising that she would make sure Sam had a hot bath straight away. Kate stared unseeing through the window as the visitors began to stream away in their cars.

She heard the study door open and turned, expecting to see Sam, but instead Jay, his hair still damp from a shower, filled the opening.

'Is she all right?' she asked anxiously.

'Fine. Sam is the least of your worries right now, Kate,' he said, with a slightly barbed edge to his voice. 'Nancy has our heroine in charge. She's having a bath and then she'll have tea with the rest of the staff. The doctor gave her the once-over, and she's apparently none the worse for her soaking.'

'I suppose I should thank you for pulling her out of the lake.'

'Instead of berating me like a fishwife in front of the assembled crowd? How very gracious of you,' he said with a touch of asperity, and she had the grace to blush. 'But I'm sure she could have managed. If she's anything like you,' he said with feeling, 'I would stake my life on it.'

'She's tougher than me, Jay. She's had to be.'

'Perhaps you should tell me?'

'No.' She tried to turn around and sit up, but he scooped up her legs and sat down alongside her, dropping her feet into his lap. He began to knead them, very gently.

'It might help.' He regarded her steadily. 'Why don't you start with the reason for your duplicity?'

She kept her eyes firmly fixed on her hands. There could be only one reason for that and she was sure he knew it as well as she did. 'I . . . ' She couldn't go on.

'Is it so hard to admit, Kate?'

She stared at him. Could she admit to an overwhelming desire that she had felt quite unable to hold in check? She was sure that was what he expected to hear. That would be easy compared with the reality that now stared her full in the face.

It couldn't be true. She didn't like him. She loathed his horrible cynical attitude to women . . . She began to shake and then, the final humiliation,

201

she burst into tears and somehow she was in his lap with his arms around her and she was sobbing on to his shoulder.

'She could have drowned and it would all have been my fault. If I hadn't started this stupid deception . . . ' She sniffed. Jay produced a handkerchief and she blew her nose. She looked up. 'I never meant it to go so far, please believe me . . . ' She stopped as he began to pull the pins from her hair and it tumbled down around her shoulders. 'What are you doing?' she demanded.

'What I should have done weeks ago. Make love to you.'

'No! You can't . . . '

'No? How are you going to stop me? There's no fictitious lover to hide behind now, Kate. You're going to have to accept the truth.' He laced his fingers through her hair, holding her face in his strong hands and looked at her for a long time. No one had ever looked at her with that fierce intensity, that determination. It was glorious and terrifying all at once.

'Don't,' she begged. 'Don't look at me like that.'

He smiled slowly. 'I'll stop if you ask me to kiss you,' he promised.

'I . . . I can't!' she said, on a little gasp.

His eyes darkened and became fierce. 'You're going to have to, my darling. I gave you my word that I wouldn't kiss you again until you asked me. I'd really hate to break it.'

Her heart was pounding crazily. She felt like a wanton lying in his arms and she was loving it. A slow smile deepened the corners of her mouth. 'But you would,' she murmured. He was gently massaging the back of her neck and she was finding it very difficult to concentrate on anything but the intoxicating pleasure emanating from his fingers. He was so close that she could see tiny gold flecks in his eyes.

'Ask me,' he insisted. His voice was compelling and she was beyond help. She lifted her hand and tentatively drew the outline of his mouth with the tip of her finger.

'Kiss me, Jay,' she murmured, and sighed as his lips touched the delicate lilac-veined lids of her eyes.

'Like that?' he asked.

'Yes,' she urged throatily. Gentle butterfly kisses trailed across the finely modelled bones of her cheeks, her nose, her chin. Then he raised his head and looked at her once more.

'Ask me, Kate. I want to hear you say it again.'

'Kiss me, Jay,' she repeated, her voice hoarse with something she hardly understood, but recognised as a need as old as man. 'Please.'

He groaned softly and laid siege to her mouth in a manner so determined that every other thought was driven from her mind. He had kissed her before and she had thought herself lucky to escape with her senses intact. But not like this. It had never been like this. She had stopped fighting him, stopped fighting herself and he took his time, teasing her mouth with light caressing touches that set a slow fire

burning deep within her. As her lips parted under his expert probing, a long, shuddering sigh escaped her; she was incapable of more and she was lost as his tongue stroked along hers and his mouth moved more urgently against her own.

She was dimly aware of his hand releasing the buttons of her blouse, but the urgent stab of a far deeper longing as he cupped her breast in his hand and began to tease an erect and sensitive nipple between his finger and thumb sent almost unbearable sensations of pleasure rippling through her body and she cried out, arching against him in an explosion of longing. He lifted his head, his eyes dark with arousal, and he drew in a sharp breath, gathering her up into his arms and rising swiftly to his feet.

'Not here,' he grated. 'There are too many people about for this . . . ' And as if to reinforce his words the door swung open and Sam stuck her head around it.

'Kate?' She saw her sister in Jay's

arms. 'What's the matter?' she demanded. 'Has she fainted? I do that when I get over-excited.'

Kate, her cheeks aflame, fumbled, all thumbs, with her buttons as she struggled to her feet. 'I'm all right now,' she said a little raggedly. 'But you gave me the fright of my life.'

'You shouldn't worry so much.' She grinned at Jay, obviously recovered from her soaking. 'I don't believe I thanked you properly for rescuing me.'

'Quite adequately,' he assured her, his voice lacking its usual urbanity. 'Where are you going, Kate?'

'I have to see about dinner. Nancy has the evening off.' Her eyes begged him to let her go.

'Don't bother tonight. We'll all go out.'

★ ★ ★

Kate and Jay were both too deeply immersed in their own thoughts to be great company, but Sam kept Tisha Maynard amused telling her about her

206

dancing, cruel in her mimicry of her teachers as only the young could be. Neither of them seemed to notice how quiet the other two were.

'I hate to break up the party,' Jay said, after a while. 'But I have a plane to catch.'

On the way home Sam plagued him with questions about his visit to the States until Kate told her to be quiet.

'I wish I could go to America,' Sam said wistfully.

Jay shook his head. 'Believe me, Sam, if there was any way I could get out of going I would.'

Later, they stood in the shadows of the courtyard and Jay held Kate, lightly, barely touching her as if to touch her would make it too unbearable to go. 'I'll be back the minute I can get away.'

'I'm not going anywhere, Jay.' He kissed her, tenderly, sweetly, and then left her there in the darkness. When she heard the car drive away, she turned towards the woods. There was no rush. She needed a little time. Time to become used to her acceptance that she wanted Jay Warwick as much as he wanted her. Perhaps more, but he must never know that.

'Enter these enchanted woods, you who dare.'

She murmured the words softly to herself. She was ready for the enchanted woods. Ready to dare. The sort of love she felt for Jay only happened once in a lifetime and she had stopped trying to run away from it.

And she was going into the relationship with her eyes wide open. Jay had never been serious about a woman in his life and she wasn't fooled into believing that he loved her. She remembered the cynical manner of his first pass at her. Women usually fell into his lap like ripe plums. It was as predictable as rain at Ascot. He smiled and they came running. Only she hadn't. She hadn't been prepared to play and that had intrigued him. Brought her more sharply into focus.

David had taught her one important lesson. No one was interested in taking on a woman who had the expensive responsibility of a younger sister. Expensive financially and emotionally. He had been cruel. But the point was well made. As long as she remembered that, she was safe from self-delusion. And if, in the end, Jay Warwick broke her heart, it could hardly be worse than the lump of ice she had carried inside her for the past three years.

★ ★ ★

Sam had been lodged in the old nursery suite on the top floor. Kate had never been up there before and, thrilled with the collection of old toys she had found, ideas bubbling for extending the open area of the house, she went in search of Tisha Maynard.

'You see!' She wound up an automaton, a monkey playing cymbals.

'Good lord! I'd forgotten all about this stuff. I think we'd better have someone down to look at it. Jay might want to sell it.'

'Sell it!' Kate was horrified. 'But we can put this back together like an old Victorian nursery. People will pay to come and see it!'

Lady Maynard looked doubtful. 'I don't know. The formal rooms are hardly ever used by the family but this is very personal.' She looked around and sighed. 'Jay was the last baby to use this nursery.'

'Jay?' Kate asked.

She laughed. 'It is rather difficult to think of him as a baby, isn't it? And perhaps he did grow up too fast, with too many responsibilities. His mother ran off with a wealthy South African, you know. My brother was killed in a plane crash out in the bush, chasing after her.'

'Oh, but that's terrible.' And perhaps explained something of his attitude to women. His belief that they were incapable of love. For an abandoned child, it must have seemed like that, especially when he was old enough to understand.

'Of course he'd led her to believe she would have a life of ease in a great house,' Tisha Maynard went on. 'The reality must have come as something of a shock. But it is not so very surprising that Jay is somewhat cynical about women.' She tried a top and it whirled furiously. 'He wasn't quite so bad when he was young. He didn't remember his mother, so I suppose her desertion hadn't felt so very *personal*. But then, when he was just beginning to be successful, he met Sally Richmond. He gave her her first chance in television.'

Kate frowned. 'She went to America, didn't she?'

'Yes. Once Jay had made her a star. But the Americans offered her the moon as well.' She sighed. 'He was away, negotiating a deal for his programmes in the Far East. The first he heard of it was in the newspapers. And he didn't even have the satisfaction of suing her for breaking her contract.' She looked at Kate. 'They had been living together for over a year and you don't have a contract with your lover, do you?' She closed the toy cupboard.

So there it was. Money, power and ambition. Sally Richmond had been offered it and hadn't even waited to say goodbye. Her hands clenched into tight little fists as she dwelt on the pain and humiliation he must have felt.

Tisha Maynard glanced around. 'Perhaps you're right about the nursery. It's silly to be sentimental. I'll mention it to Jay when he gets back.'

That evening a restlessness seized Kate and in an effort to tire herself she wandered in the park until it was too dark to see. She tried to watch television but nothing seemed to get through to her. Even a soak in a hot bath had no effect. She was jittery, too jumpy to settle to anything, and even as she prepared for bed she knew she wouldn't sleep.

She regarded her pyjamas with despair. She thought of the glamorous Annabel Courtney and wondered what she would wear in bed. She pulled a face. Something slinky in satin, no doubt. Horribly expensive. Unlike her pyjamas, rejects, bought in a sale to keep her warm and save on the heating bills, and far too large. She kicked off the legs, cinched in the waist and posed in front of the mirror, pouting provocatively.

'Hussy!' she scolded her reflection and replaced the trousers and rolled up the legs. Then she sighed. Perhaps it was time to try some hot milk.

The church clock struck one as she made her way along the galleried hall to the front stairs. There was something spooky about the back stairs after dark. At the creak of a floorboard under her foot she stiffened and then she laughed at her own foolishness. She was outside Jay's room; she heard the same sound every night when he came to bed. Now she glanced curiously at the door.

The lateness of the hour, the small sounds as the old house settled for the night, her own edginess, were all acting on her strangely and before she knew what she was doing her hand was on the gleaming brass doorknob and she was inside.

She stood for a moment, leaning back against the door, her heart pounding violently at her own boldness. Then she reached for the light switch and in the soft illumination of a tall Chinese lamp she examined her surroundings. The walls were richly panelled in oak, and heavy velvet curtains were looped back, revealing the tall mullioned windows dark against a moonless sky. There was a stone fireplace with high-backed chairs either side, and a red and blue oriental rug lay before the hearth. She took in every detail, until finally there was nowhere left to look except at the bed.

It was a huge four-poster, hung with embroidered drapes that might have been there for centuries.

The matching embroidered cover had been turned down in seeming invitation and, her heart beating hectically, Kate moved towards it and her hands stroked the cool linen sheets.

They were scented with the wind that blew from the sea and she sat on the edge of the bed and laid her head against the pillow. It was cool to her temple, balm to her sleepless, hectic thoughts. For a moment she didn't know whether she would run or stay. Then her eyelids flickered heavily and she kicked off the overlong pyjama legs and slipped between the sheets.

★ ★ ★

He woke her with a kiss. For a moment confusion and strangeness caused her heart to hammer fearfully. She tried to sit up, but the heavy cover hampered her. Then he whispered her name and it was all right. Everything was just as it was meant to be.

'Hello, Kate.'

He was leaning over her in the lamp-light, sitting on the edge of the bed, and she smiled up at him sleepily.

'Hello, Jay. Did I fall asleep?'

'Yes, darling, you were asleep. I came

back a day early to surprise you.' His face was grave. 'It seems you were one jump ahead of me. Thank you for warming my bed.' A smile twitched at the corners of his mouth and she sat up then, embarrassment at what she had done covering her with confusion.

'Oh, grief . . . ' She pushed back the cover and swung her legs to the floor. There was a gratifyingly sharp intake of breath as his eyes took in her tousled hair, the pyjama jacket twisted provocatively about her, before travelling the length of her long bare legs. 'I didn't think — '

'Didn't you, Kate?' he asked softly. 'Try not to think some more.' His lips were warm and sweet, blotting out the danger she had walked into without a thought. His hands slid upwards beneath the schoolboy stripes of her pyjama jacket, fingers spread to encompass her back, thumbs brushing against the soft mounds of her breasts and rousing an instant response that left her gasping.

Her name caught on his breath and

he bore her urgently down on to the bed. For a moment they were locked together in a world where only his lips curving a trail of fire across her throat, the weight of his body pinning her to the sheets, had any meaning.

He lifted his head and stared at her a little fiercely. 'I've missed you,' he said almost, she thought, with surprise.

She didn't answer, but began to undo the buttons of his shirt, concentrating hard on each one, conscious that he was watching her through eyes eclipsed by half-lowered lids. When it was done, she laid her hands against the hard plane of his chest, against the dark sprinkling of hair and then, a little shyly, she slid her arms up and wrapped them around his neck, leaving herself open to him, offering herself with complete trust. 'Love me, Jay,' she murmured.

For a moment she waited, hardly sure what to expect, only aware of the tremor of anticipation centred some-where about her abdomen, a touch of fear, a touch of excitement, above all, the knowledge that he would make her a total woman.

He reached up and caught her hands, bringing them to the front, holding them fast together. Then he sat up abruptly. 'You'd better go, Kate,' he said, a sudden intensity lighting the depths of his eyes.

A kind of madness had carried her across the threshold of his room, that same madness kept her pinned now to the bed. 'And if I don't want to?' She lay completely motionless as he stared at her, his eyes slowly travelling the length of her body. Then he closed his eyes.

'Please go, Kate,' he grated. 'Now.'

Ashen-faced, Kate rolled from the bed and ran for the door. Rejection was the last thing she had expected, but she should have known. This bed was sacrosanct. It would one day be for his wife. Not the place for casual affairs. 'Kate!' His voice stopped her in her tracks and expecting him to come after her, suggest an adjournment to her room, she grabbed at the door-handle, determined to get away before the insult left his lips. 'You've forgotten something.'

'What?' Bemused, she half turned.

He walked slowly across the room to her and placed the pyjama trousers in her hand. 'Goodnight, Kate. Sleep well.' He opened the door for her and stood back to let her through. With a groan of anguish she ran to her own room to throw herself on the bed and cry hot tears of shame.

* * *

Jay slept most of Friday. Nancy reported that he seemed to be more than usually jet-lagged when she took up a tray late in the afternoon. Kate raised a bleak smile and slammed down the dough she was kneading with unnecessary force.

He finally appeared just before dinner and found her alone in the kitchen. He came up behind her and put his arms around her. 'Hello, Kate,' he murmured softly in her ear.

'Hello, Jay,' she said briskly, and tried to push past him.

He held her, preventing her escape. 'That's not the standard of welcome I expected after last night.'

'I would rather forget last night.'

'Am I to read from this sudden frostiness that you regret your somewhat reckless application for the position as my bedwarmer?'

'It's not much of a job, is it?' she said icily. 'You warm a man's bed and then he throws you out of it.'

'There are a few formalities to be got through first, Kate,' he said.

'Don't put yourself to any trouble, Jay.' She stared pointedly at his hands clasped around her waist.

'The greater the trouble, the sweeter the reward. Remember?' He released her, lightly touching her cheek with his fingers. 'I'll go and see Tisha. Maybe she'll be pleased to see me.'

* * *

'Did you phone your office, Jay?' his aunt asked, as she shook out her napkin. 'They've been ringing you all day.'

'Monday will do.' He glanced at Kate. 'I've other things on my mind.' And the conversation was monopolised by Sam, who wanted to hear all about America.

In the middle of dinner there was an urgent peal at the front door and Sam went to answer it. She came back a few moments later.

'It's a courier with a package for you, Jay. The man says you must sign for it personally.'

Jay frowned and threw down his napkin. 'Can't they manage without me for a few days?' He returned a few moments later and threw the padded envelope on the sideboard.

'Tell me about your week, Sam. Have you had a good holiday?'

'Wonderful.' Her eyes sparkled. 'I've

learned how to cast a fly.'

'I'm impressed.' He raised an ironic brow. 'Did you catch anything?'

She looked stunned. 'I couldn't actually *kill* anything,' she said, horrified at the suggestion. She babbled on, amusing Tisha, filling the silence between Kate and Jay.

Finally, Jay excused himself. 'If you're making coffee, Kate, perhaps you would be kind enough to bring some to the study. I want to discuss some changes I have in mind for the future.'

'Yes, of course.' Her voice was a little unsteady. Perhaps she was over-sensitive to the atmosphere, but that sounded ominously like a prelude to dismissal.

Kate cleared the dishes and carried the coffee through to the study. She placed the tray on the table in front of the sofa and shut the door. Jay was staring at something on the desk in front of him. A newspaper clipping. Even upside down she could see that it was a photograph of them both, taken on Saturday. They were standing very close. Jay's trousers were clinging mud-dily to his legs and he was grasping her firmly by the arm. His expression was not exactly happy. He had been trying to get her away when the photographer had snapped them together after Sam's mishap at the lake.

He looked up and she froze at the hard implacability of his face. 'This is all very interesting, Kate. Perhaps you'd care to offer an explanation?' He tossed the newspaper clipping across the desk and sat back. 'Well?' he demanded. 'I'm waiting.'

8

The quiet menace in his voice was like a pain scything through her and she stepped sharply back, but the headline seemed to leap out after her, an accusation.

'Kate Unmasked', it read.

While we've all been racking our brains to discover the identity of Jay Warwick's mysterious new lady, the Kate whose name he let slip recently, the answer has apparently been lying under our noses, week after week on the women's page. It seems that the country's most elusive marriage prize has fallen for home cooking. Our own Kate Thornley, writer of delicious recipes and a superb cook, is being hotly pursued by the good-looking chairman of Magnum Television. Although, from the evidence of this photograph, not with his usual success.

Kate's column has been especially interesting lately. Apparently her country cousin Cathy has taken over the job for a while, but reading between the lines it doesn't take much imagination to work out who the chauvinistic Jack Wessex might be, especially when we learn that Kate is at present working in a large country house in Norfolk.

Annabel Courtney had better polish up her baking skills if she has any serious plans to become chatelaine of Fullerton Hall.

Photocopies of her column, dozens of them, back to her first tentative offerings two years earlier, were littered about his desk. But a few, the most recent, were marked with vivid slashes of highlighter. His staff had done their work very thoroughly. Kate didn't read them. She didn't need to. All those suggestive little remarks of Jay's had found their way into her weekly 'letters'. In the beginning, she had taken some pleasure from her small and totally private joke at his expense. Now, seeing it like this, as he must be seeing it, it seemed nothing less than a betrayal.

She stood motionless in the pool of light cast by the desk lamp and waited for the explosion, but when he spoke his voice was aloof, distant. Quite terrifying.

'Well, Kate. You'll have some really exciting copy for your paper this week, won't you?' he said. It would have been so much easier if he shouted. She could bear that, could understand that. She could shout back. But this mind-numbing display of self-control was paralysing.

She didn't answer. There was no point. He would never believe anything she said and who could blame him? How in honesty could she excuse herself? He had decided to prove a point, prove that she could not resist him. And she had retaliated. It had started as a game. But it had become so much more.

'You will remember, darling, when you're writing your poisonous little barbs, to mention that you were the one waiting in *my* bed?' There was frost-bitten white about lips. 'That no one dragged you screaming and kicking from the servants' quarters?' The words dripped like icicles into her heart, splitting it in two. She had thought she would be able to manage when he broke her heart. She was wrong. Desperately wrong. 'No need to mention that I declined your generous offer. I do have a reputation to maintain. But then, you don't have more than a passing acquaintance with the truth, do you?'

She considered the possibility of trying to explain, to justify herself, and dismissed it in the same thought. He was far too angry to listen. 'I'll go as soon as you can get a replacement,' she said dully, and turned to leave.

'No.' The word was final, not to be argued with. 'I'll handle this in my own way. And you will do exactly as you're told. Sit down.' He lifted the telephone receiver and punched in a number. 'But first, I'll have to put a stop to their nasty little innuendoes.'

'Can you do that?'

'I have it in my power to limit the damage. Newsroom, please.' He regarded her stonily. 'Have you any idea what you have brought down about our ears, Kate? Jay Warwick finds his perfect girl, a cook who's good in bed. Every column will be running with it for weeks. It's a gift of a story.'

'You've flaunted it as your ideal often enough,' she said bitterly. 'Can you blame them?'

'No, Kate, I don't blame them. They're just doing their job. But I never intended . . . Good, God, can't you see? You work in my house. I pay you a salary! At rather more than the going rate in this part of the world, I can assure you. After that last piece there are quite obvious implications . . . ' The colour drained from her face and she sank into the chair. He nodded grimly.

'Have you thought what it will do to Sam?'

'Sam?' Her head snapped up. 'What on earth has she got to do with this?'

He ignored her. 'Newsroom? Jay Warwick. I have a late item for the evening news.' He listened for a moment. 'This will go in at the end. After so much gloom, I'm sure the public will welcome a little joy. I'm announcing my marriage to Miss Kate Thornley.' He listened and grimaced, glancing across at her. 'Yes, that Miss Thornley.'

'No.' She shook her head, the chair toppled as she stood up, falling over with a crash, and she backed away, only stopping when she felt the door at her back.

He broke off at her cry, daring her with his eyes to interrupt further. 'The wedding will take place a week from tomorrow.' A sudden burst of excitement from the other end of the phone made him wince. 'If you can get a crew out from Norwich you can have some

229

live pictures. And Geoff — it's exclusive. Don't tell anyone else. Don't even tell the news team why you're sending them. I don't want any eager stringers ringing their contacts on the nationals. I want the papers left flat-footed.'

She was pressed hard against the door when he dropped the phone back into its cradle and strode towards her.

'Well?'

Kate opened her mouth to protest and then closed it again. She had long since realised that there was a lot more to Jay than the careless playboy image he liked to project. There had to be more to a man who had built on a satire show put together by a group of university students and turned it into a television empire. Much more.

In the last few moments she had seen the other side of Jay Warwick. A totally ruthless man who would stop at nothing to get his own way.

She groaned. 'Please don't do this to me. I can't . . . can't pretend that I'm going to marry you just to prevent a bit of gossip.' She wrapped her arms about herself and hung on. 'Why are you doing this?'

'Don't you know, Kate?' His eyes were unwavering. 'No. I don't believe you do.' His mouth tightened. 'Everyone loves a lover. Anything your nasty little rag prints now will just seem petty and a little bit tacky. They will understand that perfectly well and print their joyous felicitations, along with the suggestion that they engineered the whole thing.'

'It's impossible.'

He ignored this cry from her heart. 'I don't know exactly what you expected to gain from all this, Kate.' His gesture took in the desk littered with newspaper clippings. He looked down at her. 'I remember you telling me about your cookery column. I suppose I should have taken more notice. But you have a way of distracting me.' He reached out and trailed his fingers along her throat. She tried to back away, but the door was behind her and he was in front.

231

Much too close. 'You write very well. The caricature of me is done with a delicate hand.'

'Jay, believe me, I never intended — '

He ignored her appeal. 'Sadly, Sam is the one who would suffer most from the fun the press would enjoy at our expense. Between us we can save her from that. If you're the loving sister you profess to be you'll smile and look happy.'

'I won't go through with this charade, Jay.' She tried to move away, but his hand held her firm.

'What charade?' His mouth caressed her lips, emphasising the power he had to hold her, bind her to him. She shivered and apparently satisfied, he raised his head in order to press the point home. 'I urge you to consider the consequences if you don't. At the very least I shall have to take out an injunction against your newspaper — '

'On what grounds?' The words jerked from her as she suddenly saw red. Her voice was rising and she made an effort to regain control of it. 'I wrote nothing but the truth, after all!'

'Really?' He took her arm and hauled her across the room to his desk. He picked up one of the photocopies by the corner as if closer contact might contaminate him. 'This is truthful?' he asked and read from the paper. '' . . . One last thing, Kate. Mr Jack keeps asking me for something called *droit de seigneur*. I've looked it up in every cookbook I can find but it's not there. If you know what it is perhaps you could send me the recipe. You know I like to keep him happy . . . '' He shook the paper under her nose. 'Perhaps you would remind me exactly when I demanded your presence in my bed as my right? Last night you were waiting for me and I take a little comfort from the fact that I had the good sense to throw you out.' Her hand struck him before she knew what she was about, rocking him back on his feet.

'Why don't you ask Mike Howard?'

she demanded. 'He remembered your conversation with startling clarity. When he saw me in the post office he almost took to his heels and ran!'

'I haven't a clue what you are talking about.' He moved his jaw carefully. The print of her hand was livid against his skin.

'Then you'd better ask him to jog your memory!'

She turned to go. The determination that was keeping the tears behind gritty lids was almost exhausted. But his voice stayed her, harsh as it had not been throughout the whole appalling scene.

'By tomorrow the press will have found out this telephone number. I'm surprised, quite frankly, that it's taken them so long. They'll want to talk to you. I can protect you here, Kate, but then they'll get to Sam. She was in the paper too. It won't take them long to connect the names. She goes back to school in a couple of days.' He regarded her dispassionately. 'Do you want that? Reporters waiting outside the gate,

climbing over the fence, lying in wait to take photographs.' Numb, unable to utter a word, she shook her head. 'No. And neither will the school. No matter how talented she is.' Sure now of her undivided attention, he issued his instructions.

'We will go across the hall now to break the happy news to Tisha and Sam. By happy coincidence I have a bottle of champagne cooling.' She saw the ice-bucket on the sideboard and frowned, but he gave no further explanation. Instead he continued to issue his orders. 'You will go and change into something suitably festive. That red dress you wore the other night will be perfect. You'll want to look good for the television cameras, I'm sure.' He seized her face in his hands and with his thumbs wiped fiercely at the tears that were now falling unchecked down her cheeks. 'Don't do that!' he grated. Then his mouth twisted in a mocking little smile. 'Any tears on display tonight had better look as if they are tears of

happiness, don't you think?'

She made it, somehow, through the ordeal of telling Tisha Maynard and Sam. Jay did all the talking and although his aunt looked at Kate rather hard for just a moment, she was plainly delighted with the news.

'I couldn't be more pleased, my dear,' she said warmly, as Sam threw her arms about her sister and hugged her and Kate curled up inside with misery at the deception.

'The television crew will be here in a few minutes so if you'll excuse us we'd better go and make ourselves look presentable.'

Alone in her room Kate began to shake. She had stripped off her clothes and washed away the tearstains. She looked deathly pale, but now her hands wouldn't hold the make-up steady. A tap at the door and Jay's voice sent the bottle smashing into the sink.

She was hanging on to it, kneeling, her cheek against the cold porcelain when he appeared in her bathroom

door. He seized her and hauled her to her feet.

'I can't. I can't do it,' she sobbed.

He dumped her in a chair in front of her dressing-table and searched quickly through her make-up. She sat trembling violently as he flicked a blusher over her cheeks.

'That's a bit better. Close your eyes.' He made an impatient sound. 'For goodness' sake, Kate. I'll poke you in the eye with this thing if you don't stop shaking.'

'I c-c-can't h-h-help it!'

'All right. It's done. Dress?' She didn't answer and he wrenched open the door and pulled out the red silk dress. 'Stand up,' he ordered and she was beyond doing anything else. He slipped the dress over her head and zipped up the back. Quite the expert. Clearly he'd had years of practice. She used the thought as a cudgel to beat down the sensations that, despite everything, his nearness provoked in her. He pushed her feet into her shoes and turned her around. 'Just some lipstick. But first,' he said with determination, 'something for those shakes.' He jerked her hard into his arms and, despite her stiff resistance, he kissed her fiercely, his teeth grating against her tight clamped lips. For a moment there was no reaction, then a flash of anger ignited deep inside her and she began to fight him. He hung on until she savagely kicked his shin and, free at last, stood glaring at him, her chest heaving, her cheeks hectic. He regarded her impassively, completely unmoved by her fury. Then he nodded. 'That's more like it.' He tossed her the tube of lipstick. 'Here. But frankly I don't think you need it now.' The little gilt cylinder hit the door as he closed it behind him. She turned and stared at her reflection in the mirror, rubbing furiously at her swollen lips.

But the anger had brought her back to life and carried her through the worst of the press call. They stood, she and Jay, arm in arm for all the world to see in the great drawing-room at Fullerton Hall, while Jay explained how they had met over an Aga and he had fallen in love instantly. So convincing was he that, if she hadn't known better, she would have believed every word of it.

There was a slightly sticky moment when the interviewer asked Kate what she thought about the *Evening Mail*'s coverage of their romance.

'*Evening Mail*?' She looked puzzled. 'I'm sorry. I haven't looked at a paper for days.' She raised her eyes to Jay. He wasn't the only one who could act. 'I've been much too busy.' She was unaware of the delicate blush that darkened her cheeks, and only by the slightest upward movement of his brow did Jay acknowledge her performance.

The broadcast over, Jay invited the crew to share a glass of champagne with them. He turned back to Kate and refilled her glass. 'I see you've fully recovered,' he murmured, adding ominously, 'And make no mistake, my darling. I plan to see that you're kept much too busy to get into any more mischief for a long time to come.'

* ★ *

Jay was very firm that he and Kate would drive Sam back to school on Sunday. The announcement of the engagement was bound to bring in extra visitors and among them would almost certainly be reporters trying to snatch an opportunist photograph or speak to Kate.

'But Nancy shouldn't be left to cope by herself!' Kate protested.

'Why not? If you were given the chance you'd leave here like a shot. At least this way she believes she's aiding true love. When we're married she'll be doing far more anyway. But if you're worried you can always get up a little earlier and make certain everything is ready for her.'

'But we're not getting married. That was just to stop . . . ' He couldn't mean to go ahead with it. It was ridiculous. 'Jay?'

'The announcement will be in *The Times* on Monday.'

* * *

On Sunday morning she rose long before daylight to prepare as much as she could in advance.

It was still warm, with no sign of a break in the weather, although the air had become heavy. Kate felt drained and headachey and was dreading the long drive to school with Sam.

She had already written a letter of resignation to her editor, asking her to send her fee direct to a children's charity. She didn't blame the woman for what had happened. It had been her own fault entirely, but clearly she was unable to continue to work for them. The letter was lying on her dressing-table and she planned to put it in a box somewhere on the way.

There was a knock on her bedroom

door and she opened it. Jay stepped inside and closed it behind him, standing in front of it barring her escape. 'What do you want?' she asked nervously, backing off under his scouring eyes. 'How long are you going to keep me a prisoner here, Jay?'

'Prisoner?' He gave a short, harsh laugh. 'For the moment we're both prisoners, Kate, and on trial by media.' His eye fell on the letter and he frowned. 'What's this?'

'My resignation. I can't write for the *Mail* any more.'

He picked the envelope up. 'I think that would be a mistake. A final episode is required. You mustn't leave your readers in suspense.' He tapped the envelope against his hand, then pocketed it. 'It's time for Cathy to discover what *droit de seigneur* really means, don't you think?'

She ignored the threat. 'Really? And then what? Will the satisfied Jack Wessex marry her off to the gardener?'

He looked thoughtful. 'It's your

story, Kate. It's up to you. Perhaps she'll perform so well in bed that she never has to go near a kitchen again.' His knuckles whitened as he grasped the doorknob. 'Come on, let's get Sam back to school.'

★ ★ ★

Sam's arrival at school was something of a triumph. She attracted envious glances from friends and some were bold enough to ask for Jay's autograph. Kate knew she was the object of similar scrutiny from assembled mothers and sisters. What, they seemed to be thinking, can such a man see in her? He slipped his arm possessively around her shoulder as they stood chatting to a group of girls, and when he looked down at her he seemed to be answering them.

'Are you going to be a bridesmaid, Sam?' one of the girls asked. Sam looked at Kate, her eyes begging her to say yes.

'Of course she is,' Jay said, filling the silence. She stared up at him. It was cruel, but then, she could hardly blame him for taking every opportunity that presented itself to twist the knife. She knew she deserved it. She had broken her own rules and fallen in love. She had given him the power to hurt her. She had thought David's rejection when she needed him so badly had been painful. But she could never have truly loved him. She looked at his hand, the way his long fingers were locked possessively through hers. This was pain.

They received a message from the principal, asking them to join her for tea, and Kate received her felicitations with every outward sign of pleasure and Jay assured the woman that he would be delighted to watch the school's Christmas performance.

Finally it was time to leave and he settled her in the front seat of the car and drove in thoughtful silence for a couple of miles until he pulled up beside a small row of shops and produced her envelope from his pocket. 'There's a postbox.'

Kate ignored the envelope. 'Forget it,' she said with studied lightness. 'As you said, Cathy's story is incomplete.' She was still smarting at his casual use of Sam as a weapon to beat her with.

For a moment he stared at the stiff white square. Then he opened the car door and walked quickly across to the box and Kate flinched as the envelope dropped with a hollow thunk.

* * *

Shopping for a wedding-dress was a strange experience. The problem was that Kate couldn't take it seriously. She knew it wasn't going to happen. He was just drawing it out to the last minute. She was certain that Tisha must know, be part of the conspiracy to inflict the maximum pain, as she organised the details of the wedding, organised bridesmaids and flowers. Not that she betrayed, by

245

one word out of place, that she was anything but delighted. But she had known about Sam too, and kept her own counsel.

The two of them went into Norwich to buy a wedding-dress and Kate obediently tried on the dresses that were brought for her while Tisha made suggestions and pulled faces and finally beamed.

'That's perfect, Kate. Absolutely you.' The simple ivory silk gown was cut in a princess line that emphasised her slight figure and added a little height. The stiff collar stood away from the neck, giving a faintly medieval air, an illusion reinforced by wide sleeves that folded back from her narrow wrists.

'Will she want a veil?' The saleswoman had quickly realised that Tish was the one to do business with.

'I don't think so. She has such a beautiful neck that it seems a pity to hide it.' They discussed the matter at length and decided finally, without bothering her for an opinion, that her hair should be braided about her head with ribbons. She tried on shoes, regarding the silk pumps with disinterest while they argued about flowers, finally settling between them that she should carry a single long-stemmed rose.

Kate wrote a cheque for a horrendous amount of money with a growing sense of unreality. It wasn't happening. It wasn't going to happen. But on Friday night Sam arrived in a chauffeur-driven limousine and was rushed into Norwich to be fitted with her dress.

All too soon it was Saturday. The hairdresser came early and spent hours braiding her hair in a coronet about her head, weaving in narrow ribbons and leaving a knot of them to fall at the nape of her neck. Then she sat, letting Sam's excited chatter wash over her, waiting.

★   ★   ★

Kate had woken with a sense of dread. She had been stupid, she knew that. But had she really done anything to deserve what he was putting her through? Until Friday evening she had believed that he would come and release her from this nightmare. Perhaps he planned to inflict the most public humiliation possible and simply not show up.

She hadn't seen Jay since they had taken Sam back to school. 'I'll stay in London,' he had informed her. 'There's been enough speculation already.'

He had telephoned her every evening and asked all the right questions. And every night she had asked him to reconsider. On the Friday evening she had begged.

'If we break it off now,' he had told her, with a chill in his voice, 'it would be far worse than if we'd decided to live the whole thing down.'

'Worse for whom?' she demanded.

He didn't bother to answer. 'I'll see you tomorrow. What?' He covered the receiver and Kate heard only muffled voices for a moment. Then Jay said, 'Annabel sends her love.'

She hung up. She had no home, no job and there was Sam to consider. There was always Sam.

★ ★ ★

She had refused the loan of one of Tisha's friends to give her away. She had no male relation to take her father's place and she would stand by herself. But it felt lonely on the short drive from the house to the church without a reassuring arm to hang on to.

The car pulled up in front of the church and Tisha and Sam were there to arrange the folds of her dress and round up all the little girls from the estate who made an enchanting posse of bridesmaids, six in all, each carrying a tiny posy of yellow rosebuds, a shade or two darker than their dresses. Sam took her place behind them and the procession was ready. Tisha gave them a last look, before hurrying to take her place inside the church. The verger gave a signal and the organist let rip.

She could feel every eye upon her, caught sight of several smiling faces that she recognised. Everyone was looking at her. Everyone except Jay. She could see his broad, grey-clad shoulders, the thick, dark, well-groomed hair clear above anyone else. Then she was beside him and finally he glanced down.

'Kate?' The word was wrenched from him. She was hardly surprised. She had scarcely recognised her own reflection after the hairdresser had finished with her.

She turned and lifted her head. There was a haggard look about him that deepened the hollows of his cheeks and she looked quickly away. She didn't want to see the hunted expression in his eyes that told her only too clearly that this was all a sham. For him at least. Because for her it was real. She would never love anyone else the way she loved Jay. Once she had made her vows they would be married, and no quiet divorce when the fuss died down would ever change that for her.

When the clergyman asked if anyone knew just cause, she held her breath. Someone would shout. Someone must shout and disclose the pretence. Her heart was hammering in her throat, but the service continued and she couldn't say whether she was glad or sorry. Words were spoken, vows exchanged and her hand was placed in his. It was a large hand, comforting as he grasped her fingers. I should be noticing, she thought. I shall want to remember. When it's all over I shall want to remember this. But everything moved too quickly for her to catch up and it was no time at all before the bells were ringing and they were outside surrounded by photographers and the cameramen from the Magnum newsroom and he was kissing her for all the world to see that she was his.

Suddenly Annabel was there, stunningly beautiful, kissing her cheek. 'Keep him happy for me, Kate,' she murmured, and before she moved away she winked at Jay. For a moment Kate thought she would faint; only his firm grip held her on her feet.

Finally, though, it was over. Jay raised his top hat to the crowd gathered at the gate and walked her to the white open-topped Rolls-Royce that carried them very slowly up the drive to the front door of Fullerton Hall.

She stepped down from the car and stared up at the beautiful rose-red brick of the facade.

'Well, Mrs Warwick.' She started at the strangeness of her name. 'Shall I carry you over the threshold?' His voice was not quite steady. Before she could protest he had lifted her into his arms and was walking swiftly over the bridge. At the entrance he turned once more for the cameras. For just a moment she had thought there was something more in his voice, but it was a media show to the last and as he carried her inside she struggled to her feet. He caught her hand. 'Bear up, Kate. It will soon be over.'

Over. It would soon be over. Lunch was a blur. She couldn't think what she was doing marrying this man who only meant it to be for a few days . . . weeks . . . and who had spent the night before the wedding with another woman. She had put her hand up to stop her head aching, and Tisha was suddenly there.

'Come on, Kate. Time to change.'

They went upstairs to her room. Except it wasn't her room any more. No more hiding behind a locked door. There had been no mistaking Jay's meaning when he said he would be keeping her too busy to get into mischief. She kicked off the pretty ivory pumps and massaged her feet.

There was a tap at the door and Nancy put her head round. 'I've brought this, Kate. I saw you come up and guessed you could do with it.' She placed the tea-tray on the little table near the window.

'Oh, Nancy! Thank you. But you're a

guest today. You should be enjoying yourself.'

'Oh, I am. And if I might say so you looked really beautiful in the church.'

Tisha turned to Kate as the girl left them. 'She's right. You looked almost ethereal. When Jay looked at you I thought for a moment he was going to cry. I can't tell you how happy I am that he's found someone at last. Someone good.' A tear slid down Kate's cheek. 'My dear, whatever is the matter?'

But she didn't tell. She made up a lot of nonsense about bridal nerves and hardly sleeping all week. All of it true enough. She changed into a simple silk shirtwaist dress in a moss and turquoise print and finally the left the sanctuary of her room.

Jay was waiting at the foot of the stairs with Sam. They both turned as she came down the wide staircase and Jay stepped forward to take her hands. He had done that before. Just that gesture, and even the look about his eyes. But that was for those watching. It was important she remember that this was all for public consumption, nothing to do with love, and she forced herself to smile.

Sam, bouncing with excitement, interrupted. 'Jay says I can come and live here with you, Kate. Isn't it wonderful?' Her eyes were shining. Kate turned on him. It was one thing to make her life a misery, but to make promises to Sam that he had no intention of keeping was unforgivable.

'You'll always have a home with me, Sam. For as long as you need it,' she said, keeping her eyes fixed on his. 'Wherever that is.'

She turned and tossed her rose to the crowd, but she didn't see who caught it because her eyes were full of tears. Then he was whirling her through a cloud of confetti and out to the car. A huge bunch of balloons was tied to the rear bumper of the Jaguar and as they drove away there was a flurry of flashes as photographers took advantage of the last opportunity for a picture.

'Where are we going?' she asked finally, to break the silence.

Jay turned to her, eyebrow raised slightly. 'Does it matter?' She shook her head. Of course it didn't matter. The wedding was a nightmare, the honeymoon would be a farce. 'Kate, about Sam: I realise — '

She stared straight ahead. 'It was unkind of you to raise her hopes like that, Jay. We agreed that this is a purely temporary arrangement.'

He pulled over to the side of the road and turned to her. 'Perhaps you'd better remind me, Kate,' he said, very quietly, 'because I seem to have forgotten. Just when did we agree that this marriage was to be temporary?'

9

Startled, Kate turned to find herself the object of a pair of wintry eyes. 'I . . . We didn't . . . ' she stammered. Then fury lent her a voice. 'Of course it's temporary. We both know that. I'm your pound of flesh and perhaps I deserve what you're doing to me, but Sam doesn't.'

'Pound of flesh?' He blanched. 'Is that what you were offering the other night? You'll have to forgive me if I say something extremely vulgar, because that's the only response that fits the way I feel.' She flinched, and with an exasperated gesture he got out of the car and freed the balloons and they drifted away over a nearby hedge. She watched them as he got back into the car, not wanting to face him, or even herself. But he didn't start the engine and finally she was forced to turn. He was watching her, his eyes searching for an answer to some question that troubled him.

'This is all about Sam, isn't it? Are you determined to give up your own life for her? She wouldn't want you to. Or perhaps you're just trying to prove to the world how wonderful you are?'

'You know nothing about it,' she said dully.

'Why don't you tell me, then?' He started the engine and moved slowly away, his eyes fixed firmly on the road. 'We've a long way to go.'

'It's not very important. Only to me.'

'Tell me, Kate,' he insisted.

So she told him. 'My mother was a dancer. Nothing special. The same as hundreds of other girls. Good enough for the chorus of a musical. But I think she must have loved it. Then she met Dad and I arrived and that was the end of her glorious career.' She was unaware of the sigh that escaped her lips. 'She sent me to dance school as soon as I could walk, trying to live it all again through me, I suppose. Ballet lessons, tap, the lot. I was hopeless. No timing.' She smiled a little ruefully as she remembered. 'I'm afraid I was a great disappointment to her. Then when I was nine, she had Sam. And Sam was born dancing. Even in the baby class she shone. You should see her, Jay. It's extraordinary. When she moves to music she seems to shimmer.'

'How does she manage?' he asked. 'You can't lipread music.'

'She isn't totally deaf and she says . . .' She glanced at him, wondering if he would believe it.

'Yes?'

'She says that she can feel the music. Through her feet, the tips of her fingers. She's just incredibly sensitive to vibrations, I suppose. The school couldn't give her a scholarship, but they wouldn't have taken her unless she was outstanding.'

'Don't worry about her fees, Kate. I'll pay them.'

'I can manage,' she said, a little

fiercely. 'The money from the flat . . . '

He glanced at her sharply. 'You sold your home to pay for her to go to dancing school?' His face stiffened. 'That's why you wanted a live-in job.' He wasn't asking her a question, merely answering one of his own.

She had hardly had time to miss her parents today. Talking about her mother brought them so vividly to her mind. How much they would have loved it all today. Except if they had been alive she would have been married to David and there would have been another life altogether. For a moment she wondered what it would have been like and realised with a slight shock that she couldn't even recall his face.

'What happened to your parents?' he asked, after a while.

'They were killed in a car accident. It was foggy, Dad missed the road. But Sam was thrown clear . . . ' Her voice was shaking and she stopped until she regained control. 'At first they thought she was unhurt. Then her hearing began to deteriorate.'

Aware of disturbing painful memories, Jay left her in peace and concentrated on the long drive into London.

★   ★   ★

London should have been fun. She had lived there all her life, but it had never been like this. It began that first morning of their married life with a trip to a jeweller's.

'It's late, I know, but I thought you'd rather choose your own ring.' He laid her hand across his. 'Such slender fingers.' He kissed each one, making her blush before the serious black-clad figure of the manager. But he had missed no opportunity to flirt with her when there was someone to witness him in the act.

When she had realised he was taking her to his house in London she had been astonished and had said so.

'I thought you were desperate to avoid publicity.'

'There's publicity,' he said, his face darkening slightly, 'and there's publicity. If they want to gossip about us, we'll let them. They can have as many pictures as they like of us looking deliriously happy.' He glanced at her. 'I do realise that you're not deliriously happy, Kate, but it would help if you could make an effort. They'll soon get fed up with it, believe me. Happiness doesn't sell newspapers.'

So when he kissed her fingers, she knew it was for effect and, firmly ignoring the desperate pull of desire, she allowed him to choose a solitaire diamond for her. It was the most beautiful thing she had ever seen. She would return it to him when the charade was over, but for now she would enjoy the pleasure of seeing it on her finger and making believe to the world that everything was as perfect as the stone.

'Quite lovely, if I may say so. An excellent choice.' The jeweller managed a smile of surprising warmth and Jay regarded him with approval.

'My sentiments exactly,' he said, and raised her hand to his lips. 'Come on, Kate. It's time for you to do some shopping.'

He drove her to a boutique in Knightsbridge. 'Start here.' He handed her a list and an envelope full of banknotes. 'By the time you've finished here there'll be a car with a driver waiting for you. You have accounts at the stores on this list. Buy everything you want.'

'But, Jay . . . ' she protested.

But the teasing warmth that he had displayed for the jeweller was no longer in evidence. They were alone and he was abrupt. 'We'll be in London for at least a month and I don't want to see you in the same thing twice.'

'Jay, I can't!'

'Really? Whatever happened to 'love, honour and obey'?' he demanded.

Kate looked aghast. 'Surely no one ever uses that any more?'

'Don't you remember?' She tried to

recall the words of their wedding service. 'You weren't paying attention, were you, Mrs Warwick?' he said, rather grimly. 'You'll just have to take my word for it.'

'I —'

'I'll see you later. I've a few things to organise. And I particularly like that shimmery thing in the window. Get it.'

And because she was angry with him, when she arrived home hours later there was hardly any room left for her in the chauffeur-driven car he had sent for her.

The Spanish couple who looked after Jay at his London home had welcomed Kate with obvious delight. Now, opening the door, Maria exclaimed with excitement and called her husband to help carry the parcels into the house.

'Kate? Is that you?' Jay called to her from his bathroom.

'And who else might it be?' she demanded from the safety of her own bedroom.

'That would be telling. Come and

talk to me.' She walked through the door that joined their rooms and stood a little self-consciously on the threshold of his bathroom. He was lying back in the tub, soaking, eyes closed. 'Did you buy everything you're likely to need?' he asked.

'Yes,' she admitted. 'And a great deal I'm not.'

He opened one eye. 'Good. Tonight, Mrs Warwick, we're going to the opera. I hope you've bought something absolutely stunning to wear because you are going to be the centre of attention.'

'Am I?' Somehow the prospect of appearing in public on his arm in the stunning creation he insisted she buy was not so very displeasing.

'Well? Don't I deserve a thank-you?'

'Certainly, Jay. Thank you.'

'A proper thank-you.' He closed his eyes. 'Kiss me.'

She swallowed nervously. There was something so aggressively male about him as he lay stretched out, his arms along the edge of the huge bathtub, master of all he surveyed. Including her, although he had made no move yet to prove it.

On her arrival she had been shown to a beautiful bedroom with its own bathroom, adjoining a similar suite occupied by him. After dinner she had gone up and changed into a silk nightgown, rather like the one she had envisaged Annabel Courtney wearing, and lain in the vast bed waiting for him, her heart pounding with apprehension and nerves and something that might just have been longing if she had allowed herself to analyse the feeling. But he hadn't come.

She moved closer to the bath and gazed down at the man she loved so much that it was a pain beneath her ribs. The she leaned gingerly forward and very gently kissed his forehead. His arms caught and held her.

'That wasn't a proper thank-you. It wasn't even a proper kiss.' His eyes flashed open. As he jerked her towards him she toppled over and fell with a scream into the bath. It was some time before he spoke and when he opened his eyes again they were basalt dark. 'That, Mrs Warwick — for future reference — was a proper thank-you kiss,' he murmured, and then he released her.

Kate, for a moment lost deep in wonder as his mouth claimed hers with a savage passion, suddenly realised she had been dismissed. She scrambled from the bath, her grey eyes sparking furiously, her suit, her hair dripping on to the marble floor, and glared at him.

'I'll do my best to remember, sir,' she said and turned and walked back to her own room, slamming the door behind her.

★ ★ ★

She should have enjoyed the opera. But she didn't. Every moment she was conscious that she was on display. That his warm smile, his attentive manner, were simply to impress the people who were so eager to speak to them, to meet

Jay's new wife. Despite her finery and the fact that her hair and make-up had been done for her by a beautician who had come to the house, and the diamond choker glittering at her neck, placed there by Jay before they left the house, she felt unpolished, gauche and conscious of their eyes turned upon her, wondering.

★ ★ ★

They stayed in London for nearly five weeks. By the time they left Jay had taken Kate to every show she expressed a wish to see. They had danced at all the fashionable nightspots and dined everywhere that the rich and famous were seen. Then one evening, as they arrived at a nightclub, Annabel Courtney waved across the room and, without asking Kate whether she wanted to join them, Jay went over.

Jay danced with her, holding her close, and she tried not to tremble, to betray the longing that grew rather than diminished as he stayed away from her bed. Then Annabel's companion, heavily gallant, asked Jay if he might dance with his charming wife. Jay agreed, almost too quickly. On previous occasions when she had been asked to dance by his acquaintances, he had kept a firm hold of her hand and told them to find their own women. But she had seen Jay and Annabel exchange a glance. They wanted to be left alone and suddenly it was plain that this was no casual encounter. Annabel was getting impatient. Perhaps she should put the woman out of her misery, Kate thought, and tell her just how faithful Jay had been to his long-time lover.

She danced with the man for a while, then excused herself, saying that she wasn't feeling very well. It wasn't a lie: their table was empty and Jay and Annabel weren't dancing. She fled to the powder-room and took a while to gather herself, put the smile back in place. When she emerged she went to the door at the rear where there was a small courtyard garden, desperate for a breath of air. For a moment she thought she was alone. Then she heard the murmur of low voices. Jay and Annabel. They were standing in the shadows, very close, and she was unable to move without them seeing her.

' . . . I'm sorry to mess things up, Annie. I had to do it. Good Lord, it's only for a few weeks. Can't you manage . . . ' Her hands clenched into small tight fists, her knuckles bone-white, and her nails dug into the palms of her hands as the bitter gall of jealousy rose in her throat and threatened to overwhelm her. She wanted to fly at Annabel Courtney and scratch her eyes out. Jay Warwick was her husband. He didn't want her, that was plain, but if he could stay out of her bed, he could stay out of Annabel Courtney's . . .

She stepped forward. 'Jay? I'm tried, darling. Can we go home?' She walked across to him and slipped her arm through his, smiling up at him, resting with her eyes that sleep was the last thing on her mind.

His eyes narrowed slightly. 'I'll get your wrap.'

On the way home, he suggested it was time to go back to Norfolk. It came as something of a relief. The scene in the nightclub had been the last straw. 'Yes, it's time to get back to work.' She attempted a joke as they stood in the elegant hall of his London home. 'I need the rest.'

He held her absently, rubbed her cheek with the back of his hand. 'Poor Kate. Have I run you off your feet? I'm sorry. But it's done the trick. We've become so boring that we haven't been in a newspaper for a whole week. Now we can drop out of sight and get on with the rest of our lives. No one will even notice we've gone.' And she cried herself to sleep in her lonely bed.

★　★　★

The rest of our lives. As they headed home the phrase seemed to thrum

271

through her head. What life? A few weeks? At least if she had had an affair with Jay she would have had something to remember. Five weeks of dressing up to impress celebrity-watchers wasn't exactly her idea of life. She left most of her finery behind in London. She would have no use for it in Norfolk. No use for it ever again.

She woke in a sudden panic as the car halted. 'Jay?'

'Time to wake up, sweetheart. We're home.'

'Home?' She looked around. Fullerton Hall. Her home. At least for a while. She took the hand he offered to help her out of the car.

'Hello, Tisha,' he said, bending to kiss his aunt, who came out of the house to meet them.

'Hello, Jay.' She looked at Kate. 'How re you? Did you have a good time?' en she laughed. 'I suppose that's a id question. Of course you have. I 't stopped reading about the two in the papers. You can come and tell me all about it tomorrow when you've had time to catch your breath.' She placed a bunch of keys firmly into Kate's hand and wrapped her fingers around them. 'These are yours now.'

Kate looked desperately at Jay. 'Finally escaped to the Dower House, Tisha?'

'And about time too. I was beginning to give up hope that you would ever settle down.'

'Have you got everything you want?'

Lady Maynard beamed. 'It's bliss. Mrs Douglas and I are as comfortable as two fat bugs.'

'No!' Kate was horrified. 'No, you must stay, Tisha! This is your home.'

'Not for a million pounds, my dear. I've reached an age where I need my comforts close at hand. I'm getting too old to walk ten miles a day just to get from room to room.' She patted her hand. 'I'll leave you two young things in peace.'

'Jay . . . '

'Now you know why Tisha's been nagging me to get married for years.

273

She can't wait to hand it all over. When you're her age I dare say you'll feel the same.'

'Jay! You must tell — '

'Say goodbye, darling. You can visit tomorrow and tell her off as much as you like. Right now you can go and put your feet up. I'm sure Nancy will appreciate a little help tomorrow.'

'Nancy's staying in Oulton Market tonight, Kate. She's left you a casserole in the fridge. It just needs heating up.'

'I'll come and see you in the morning, Tisha.'

'Not before eleven,' she warned, and refused Jay's offer of a lift. 'The walk will do me good.'

Kate turned on Jay the minute they were inside. She held out the keys helplessly. 'What on earth am I supposed to do with these?'

'Lord knows,' he said, clearly bored with the subject. 'I'm sure they're purely ceremonial.'

'And when you've decided that this farce is over?'

For a moment his eyes gleamed dangerously. Then he shrugged. 'Throw them in the dustbin if you like.'

★ ★ ★

She unpacked her suitcases, stowing everything carefully away in the room she had left as a bride a few weeks earlier. It had been easy enough to keep up a pretence of marital bliss in London with adjoining rooms. She wondered what the cleaning staff would make of this arrangement. It probably didn't matter. If they valued their jobs they would keep their mouths closed.

Afterwards she heated the casserole, although she didn't feel in the slightest bit hungry. Jay disappeared into his study and, after trying to get interested in the television, Kate decided that she would go to bed and read. She had already changed into her nightdress when she realised that she had left her book in the car. She slipped on a wrap and went outside to retrieve it.

The weather had become dreadfully close in the last few days. It was so muggy that she could hardly breathe and the air had a curious metallic smell to it that gave her goose-bumps. A scurry of wind stirred the silk gown against her legs, sending a shiver through her as she hurried across to the coach-house to retrieve her book. Then she knew what was going to happen and she forgot about her book and began to run.

The sky was scorched with the unearthly flash of lightning before she made it to the house. She slammed the door and ran to the study, but Jay wasn't there. She stood in the hall, unable to think or reason and as she hesitated the first crack of thunder shook the earth. And sensible, capable Kate Warwick opened her mouth and screamed.

'Kate?' Jay appeared in the doorway of his bedroom, naked but for a towel wrapped around his waist. 'Kate? What is it?' he demanded.

She didn't answer. Was lost in blind panic as she picked up the skirt of her wrap and ran up the long staircase determined upon the safety of her bed. But Jay caught her and spun her round, holding her, his eyes creased in sudden concern.

'My God, Kate, whatever is the matter with you? You're shaking.' She balked and went rigid as the blackness of the windows behind him was lit up by forked lightning that scythed livid across the sky. A low moan escaped her lips as she waited for the dreadful sound she knew would follow. 'Kate? Tell me?' Jay shook her slightly. 'Are you ill?' The thunder cracked directly overhead and she wrenched herself free, diving for the huge four-poster that represented safety of a sort, burrowing under the covers, hiding her head beneath the pillows.

A scud of rain broke against the window-pane and Kate whimpered, shaking with terror, scarcely aware that Jay had slipped in beside her and had reached to offer her some comfort. Another crack of thunder rent the air and she pulled violently away, erupting from the covers, her hands over her ears. 'I can't bear it. Jay, please! Stop it! Make it go away!' She turned and buried her face in his warm chest and he pulled her down and covered them both with the cover, wrapping his arms around her head to cut off the terrible noise.

'Hush! It's all right. Everything will be all right.' He held her close as the storm raged around them, stroking her, raining gentle kisses about her hair and ears, cradling her as she trembled in his arms.

Gradually the storm moved away to sea and the shivering began to subside. Exhausted, she lay heavy as lead in his arms. Soon she knew she would begin to feel foolish, as she always did once the terror was passed. But right now she didn't care. She had survived and she closed her eyes and went to sleep.

She woke in unfamiliar surroundings, shadowy from the soft light of a lamp. Then she remembered and turned to find Jay, propped on his side, watching her.

'Are you all right now?' he asked.

'I'm sorry.'

'Don't be.' She gradually became aware that she was lying alongside Jay's half-naked body. It was beautiful in the soft pool of lamplight, like a marble statue she had once seen, but Jay was warm and the muscles rippled beneath his skin as he moved. And now he was looking down at her with something that might have been amusement touching his eyes. 'But I do believe that you told me a lie, Kate Warwick,' he said.

'A lie?' A shiver ran through her. Did he think that she was incapable of telling the truth?

But his hand stroked her face very gently. 'A very small one. You told me

279

you were afraid of nothing and I believed you.'

She swallowed hard. 'Except thunder. I know it's irrational. God shifting the wardrobe, that's all. I just can't help it.'

'And do you always hide under the bedclothes?'

She smiled a little sheepishly. 'Where else? You're safe there, didn't you know? Safe from monsters, safe from the dark, safe from thunder.' But that was all illusory. With Jay's arms around her she had felt a different kind of safety. Something warmer, more substantial. But his hand had strayed from the gentle comfort of her cheek. Slid hardly noticed over the smooth silk of her wrap to rest against her waist. And as he looked down at her, her body cried out for him.

'That's all rot, you know,' he murmured, and his eyes darkened as the firm ripe bud of her breast hardened, betraying her. 'Bed can be a very dangerous place indeed.' He pulled the tie of her gown and she made no protest.

He didn't rush her. Sensing that she was as nervous as a young doe, he took his time, uttering soft reassuring words as he smoothed the silk from her shoulders, nuzzling the smooth hollows of her neck until she shivered.

'Cold?' She shook her head. How could she be cold with the man she loved holding her in his arms? But suddenly the enormity of what she was about to do hit her, and she tensed.

As if sensing her uncertainty, he brushed the hair back from her face. Tender caresses of his lips covered her eyes, her cheeks, her forehead until she thought she would scream with the need for him to kiss her and her hands reached up to grasp his head and draw him down to her. Then his mouth was hard on hers, demanding, potent, hungry, and his body was pressing against her.

He cursed softly and threw back the covers. 'I want to see you,' his voice grated. 'All of you.' She moaned at this desertion, but he drew the soft silk from her body, sliding it from her ankles, over her thighs to expose the creamy length of her body, his mouth following his urgent hands with butterfly touches that made her gasp with a sort of wonder. Then he dropped the discarded gown on the floor and lifted his head to feast himself.

'You're so lovely, Kate. I don't know how I've found the strength to stop myself from doing this. Night after night . . .'

She lay back on the pillows, her hair a dark fan about her face. 'I was waiting for you, Jay. Why didn't you come?'

'Because I forced you to marry me and I didn't want you ever to say I had simply taken my 'pound of flesh'. Only once, when I had you in that bath did I come close . . .' He broke off. 'Thank heaven for thunder.' Then, with an effort of will that must have cost him dear, he turned away and lay on his back, staring up at the canopy. 'If you're not certain, Kate, if you want to go . . . it's not too late.'

She propped herself up and with one hand tugged at the towel, wrapped so firmly about his waist. It was her turn to glory in the sight of his hard lean body and her fingers seemed to know what to do, how to show him how much she wanted him. He shivered as she touched him, and whatever happened afterwards she would have this to remember. 'Yes it is, Jay. Far too late.'

He reached up and lightly touched the hard expectant peak of her breast and she writhed with pleasure, then cried out as his hand cupped it and his mouth replaced his finger.

'Jay . . . I think I should . . . ' But he moved swiftly to lay her on her back and his tongue traced a line across her stomach and curled around her navel and the words were obliterated from her mind, dwindling to a soft whimper as his hands and mouth drove her instead to beg him for the fulfilment she so urgently desired.

'Now, my love? You're ready now?'

Her demand was urgent and he did

not keep her waiting. The sharp stab of his entry was swiftly followed by almost unbearable pleasure, immersion in a world that was nothing but sensation as Jay, gently at first and then with growing ferocity, brought her to a crashing finale of ecstasy.

Afterwards he stroked her hair, holding her against his chest where she could hear his heart hammering against her ear.

'You have a job for life, Kate. Bedwarmer-in-chief. I'll have the contracts drawn up tomorrow,' he murmured.

She ignored the sharp little pinprick of pain at the words as he kissed her brow. She hadn't expected professions of undying love. There would be time enough, later, for pain. But not now. Now she was in his arms and that was all that mattered.

'I already have a contract,' she said, laughing a little shakily. 'Don't let's get carried away.'

'That contract covers cooking. It wasn't exactly what I had in mind.' He kissed her tenderly. 'Did I hurt you?'

She shook her head and blushed. 'I tried to tell you.'

He drew back and looked down at her. 'Did you think I hadn't guessed? Why did you think I wanted to wait?' He traced the line of her jaw with his mouth and she clung to him dizzily. 'You said once that I'm not your type.' He smiled lazily down at her. 'Now, in the light of your somewhat overwhelming response to me, would you care to revise your opinion?'

'You already have far too good an opinion of yourself,' she said, but softened the words with a smile.

'Not true. I know my faults. But that's not the reason you held me at bay for so long.'

'No. I suppose I've been holding the world at bay. But after David — '

'David?' He was very still. 'I thought I had successfully routed all my rivals. Then you manage to produce another man and confound me. Who is this David?'

She stiffened at the edge in his voice. 'I . . . I was engaged to him. A long time ago. That's all.'

'All?' His eyes narrowed. 'I don't think so.'

'When Mum and Dad died he made it very clear that Sam was a responsibility he couldn't handle.'

'You're not serious?'

Kate couldn't look at him. 'He said if I didn't arrange to have her fostered the wedding was off.'

A sharp sound escaped his lips. 'Then you seem to have had a lucky escape.'

'No, Jay. Sam is an expensive girl. There were always fees for dancing lessons, shoes, travelling . . . a hundred things you wouldn't dream of. And now fees for the dance school. Who would be prepared to take on that responsibility? David may have been self-centred, but he had his own life, he wanted to start a business. He may have been cruel, but he taught me a valuable lesson not to get seriously involved. I couldn't have taken that kind of rejection twice.'

'So?' he asked softly. 'What changed your mind? How was it that I found you waiting for me in my bed one night?'

She didn't want to answer that question. Had no answer to it, except that she had fallen helplessly and hopelessly in love with him. And she wasn't about to tell him that.

'I thought . . . couldn't see any reason . . . why I shouldn't take the affair that you were offering. I was the only one who would get hurt. I didn't know . . . ' She gasped as he touched her and her eyes smoked with desire.

'Well, my love, you certainly know now.'

'Yes. I do,' she said a little fiercely. She allowed her fingers the freedom to trail the outline of his shoulder. Then her tongue began its own exploring sorties, her senses drowning in the sharp scent of sweat and the taste of salt on his skin and the urgent stirring of his need for her.

'Fast learner, aren't you?' he said, pulling her down to lie on top of him.

'I have an excellent teacher.'

'The lesson isn't over yet, my darling.'

★ ★ ★

'Jay?'

'Yes, my love?' He looked up from his perusal of the morning paper and frowned. 'You haven't eaten anything.'

'I will. In a minute.'

He put his paper down and took her hand. 'What is it? Not fed up with married life already?' It was nearly six weeks since they had returned from London. If the first weeks of her marriage had been agony, since the night of the thunderstorm it had been bliss. But she had never forgotten the conversation she had overheard with Annabel. He had promised her that it would be a matter of weeks. She knew it couldn't last for much longer. And she had to know.

'No,' she said, in answer to his question. She would never tire of him, never in a million years. 'But . . . ' It was all so difficult. And her beloved Jay sitting opposite her in nothing but a towelling wrap was doing little to help her get her thoughts straight.

'Well?'

'I think we ought to settle a few things. About the future.'

He frowned. 'What things?'

'Please don't make it difficult. You know exactly what I mean. I would like to know . . . I need to know . . . ' she swallowed. 'How long are you planning to keep up this pretence at marriage?'

Only the slightest darkening along his cheekbones suggested that he might be angry. 'Are we pretending? It all seems very real to me.'

'I . . . Well . . . ' She stopped.

'Of course, you always planned that it should be temporary. I had forgotten. Well, how long did you plan our affair should last?' he prompted, a little harshly. 'Always supposing I had

succumbed to your wanton blandish-
ments.' She didn't answer. 'Or was I to
be just a one-night stand?'

Her cheeks flamed and the creases at
the corners of his mouth deepened
slightly. She looked away, unable to
bear his amusement. 'My contract is
until the end of September . . . I would
have been leaving then.'

'Your contract? Of course, it's so
obvious I should have thought of it
myself. However, I must insist on an
option to renew it . . . if circumstances
dictate.'

'What circumstances?'

He regarded her steadily. 'I'm sure
something will turn up.'

10

Kate woke early. It was still dark and for a while she lay quiet and still, listening to Jay's even breathing. She felt oddly queasy but thought that if she stayed perfectly still the feeling might go away. Then she knew it wasn't going to, and as gently as haste would allow she eased herself from the vastness of the four-poster and bolted for the bathroom.

Afterwards she stared at her reflection. How could she have been so stupid? In the week before the wedding she had been too numb to think about anything very much, let alone precautions against pregnancy, and once they were in London it had no longer mattered. She had known she was late. But there had been so many upsets, so much tension that she had allowed herself to ignore the now all too obvious truth. She touched the smooth contour of her abdomen, wondering at the miracle that was taking place within her. A baby. Hers and Jay's. She looked at herself in the mirror and her reflection smiled idiotically back.

She splashed her face with cold water. Colour was already returning to her lips but she felt weak and she returned to bed. Jay hadn't moved, but as she edged back under the cover his arm wrapped itself around her, fastening her close to him, and for a while she lay there, hugging her joy quietly to herself.

When she woke again he was standing over her, a tray in his hand. 'Come on, sleepyhead. It's nine o'clock.'

'What? It can't be.' She threw back the cover and sat up quickly. 'It's Sunday. I must get up . . .'

'Time enough. I've brought you some breakfast.'

The thought made the queasy feeling come back, but the tray contained nothing more threatening than tea and a few thin slices of toast which Jay, propping himself beside her on the bed, helped her to eat.

'Happy?' he asked, brushing back a dark wing of hair that obscured her face. 'It's important, you know, when you're having an affair, to enjoy it,' he said with absolute seriousness. 'Even when you're married to the person you're having it with. Not much point otherwise.'

'I bow to your experience in these matters.' She forced herself to make a joke of it. 'And you?'

The warm brown eyes laughed. 'I can't remember when I last enjoyed myself so much.' She felt a twinge of guilt at her own double happiness, wondering whether Jay would be quite so pleased with life when he discovered she was pregnant. Then with a painful start she realised that he must not find out or he would feel obliged to stay. This was the something that would turn up. He had realised the danger, even if she hadn't.

She loved him too much to bind him to her that way. It no longer mattered how long he was prepared to stay with her, she had her own very personal calendar. She would have to leave Fullerton Hall before he ever began to suspect.

Kate arrived in the kitchen to find everything done and waiting. In the weeks since they had returned from London Nancy had taken on more and more of the catering and now even more of the responsibility was going to fall on her. She would have to be given promotion and a rise.

'You've done wonders. I'm obviously totally surplus to requirements.'

Nancy looked horrified. 'Oh, no, Mrs Warwick. That's not true. I couldn't manage all the ordering and the books.'

Kate laughed. 'You will, you know.' She was going to have to. 'It's the next stage in your training. You can help me with it this week. But if you don't need me just now I could do with some fresh air. I'm going for a walk.' And in the quiet of the wood she decided what she would do.

She prepared an early lunch for everyone, but was then steered out of the kitchen by Nancy who insisted she could manage. She tried to read a magazine but couldn't concentrate, wondering if everything was all right in the kitchen.

'I miss that stupid dog, you know,' Jay said at last, raising his head from a book.

Kate managed a smile. 'Me too. She was always a good excuse for a walk if nothing else.'

'Why don't you get a puppy? It will be company for you while I'm gone.'

Panic stabbed through her. 'Gone?' she demanded. So soon? Surely just a week or two longer?

'I do have to work sometimes, Kate. I've rather let things slide during the last couple of months and I had a rather desperate call this morning. I have to go to London for a few days.'

On a Sunday? It took a minute to

control her breathing properly. Annabel was getting impatient. 'Of course,' she said. 'I understand. I think I might spend the time sorting out the nursery.' His eyes darted to hers and, afraid she had given herself away, she rushed on. 'It's full of old toys. I talked to Tisha about restoring it to a Victorian nursery . . . '

'She mentioned it. I don't think we should open the nursery, Kate.' He regarded her intently.

'It would be a wonderful attraction. Tisha thought so too,' she said.

'Did she?' He shrugged. 'Well, find out about it if you must.'

'I might as well make myself useful. I'll need to consult some experts though. I'm no historian.'

'Norwich Museum should be able to help, or maybe the National Trust. They must have something along similar lines.'

'I could always try Mike Howard,' she said, with a touch of irritation.

'I doubt you'll find him very reliable

as a source of information,' he said, and for a moment she thought she had managed to dent his complacency. 'But try him by all means if you think he can help.'

★ ★ ★

She found it difficult to sleep on her own. The bed was vast and she kept reaching for Jay and waking up when he was not there.

He had been away three days and although he never failed to phone at least twice each day, she missed him more than she thought it possible to miss any human being. She had always been so self-contained. Once she had broken with David she had made a point of not getting involved. Hardly difficult when she was working most evenings, and holidays had been spent with Sam. A younger sister in tow seemed to have a very dampening effect on the ardour of any potential admirer.

At least, she thought, running to the

bathroom, with Jay in London she had been able to indulge her morning sickness without the additional strain of trying to be quiet as well.

The knowledge that she was expecting Jay's baby gave her a deep happiness, despite the complications this added to an already over-complicated life. She had never imagined having a child of her own and now she treasured the secret like a miser and made her plans.

She would look for premises for a small restaurant or a catering business in East Anglia, abandoning her plans for London. She didn't want her child to grow up in a city. She had already started to look in the local papers. Not that she would buy anywhere too close; when she disappeared from Jay's life it would be for good.

She showered and dressed with the utmost care in one of her new outfits and decided to take advantage of Jay's absence to drive down to Suffolk and have a look around. Time, after all, was no longer on her side and her baby's future was more important than her own misery that Jay was in London with Annabel.

On the way back she had a sudden yearning for oranges and stopped to buy some at the vegetable stall in Oulton Market. As she took the bag she found Mike Howard at her side.

'Kate! May I offer you my best wishes?'

'Thank you, Mike,' she said with cool reserve.

'Come and have a cup of coffee. My office is just over there.'

The thought of coffee brought on an immediate attack of queasiness. 'Not coffee, Mike, thanks, but I've been meaning to telephone you. Is there anyone locally who can help me with a Victorian nursery? I'm thinking of opening the nursery wing to the public.'

'That's very enterprising of you. You're becoming a major attraction. I could probably help with some National Trust leaflets — ' he ushered her through into his office ' — and there are some books you should read. I'll look up the library index and let you have a list.'

'That would be great. Jay said you wouldn't be a very reliable source of information.' She forced a smile. 'I can't think why.'

'Well perhaps he wasn't referring to social history.' He fiddled with a pen on his desk. 'The thing is . . . Jay is rather angry with me. You see, I rather misled you, Kate. I planned to write and apologise but then suddenly you were married and it didn't seem quite the thing . . . Perhaps I can do it now?'

Kate sat perfectly still. 'Misled me, Mike? I don't follow you.'

'That day I tried to avoid you.' He looked extremely uncomfortable. 'Jay hadn't exactly warned me off. He just said that there was someone else in your life and he thought perhaps I should know.'

She placed her head on one side. 'I see. And you assumed it was Jay?'

'Well, yes. Obviously.' No, Mike, she thought. Not obvious at all. Jay had, if anything, underplayed his hand a touch, but Mike just wasn't that subtle.

She wouldn't have believed she could feel any worse about what she had done. Apparently she was wrong. Not only had she exposed Jay to unpleasant publicity, but he had been an innocent victim.

She rose. 'Perhaps you could let me have those leaflets some time?'

The telephone was ringing as she walked into the house and she picked up the receiver in the hall.

'Kate?' Jay's voice was edged with concern. 'I've been trying to get you for hours. No one seemed to know where you were.'

'I've just been having a look round. I went down as far as Beccles.'

'Well, don't. If you want to go sightseeing, wait until I can take you.'

Kate forced a light laugh. 'What is this? I don't need a chaperone.' Before he could answer she pressed on. 'I saw Mike Howard today. He's going to try and get me some information for the nursery.' Jay made no comment and she gripped the receiver. 'He explained about . . . what he said . . . '

'Did he?'

'I'm sorry, Jay. I should have known.'

'Don't blame yourself. My motives weren't that pure.' He laughed softly and her heart flipped at the sound. 'Not pure at all, in fact. I'll be home about midday tomorrow. Perhaps I could spend the afternoon demonstrating . . . ?'

'Why, sir, I don't know what you mean.' But when she carefully replaced the receiver, a tear slid down her cheek.

*   *   *

The sky was dark and overcast when she woke and it hardly seemed to be day although the clock said eight and the sun must have risen, somewhere beyond the grey. She made a pot of tea and carried it through to the sitting-room and switched on the television.

Annabel Courtney was laughing. She was leaning back on the sofa in the studio, laughing at something someone off-screen had said. It was quite preposterous that anyone who had got up at five in the morning should look that good, but then, Kate had to admit, she had everything to start with. Tall, a beautiful figure and that glorious glowing blonde hair.

The camera moved and Kate froze. Jay was leaning towards the woman, touching her arm in an almost intimate gesture. She only just made it to the cloakroom before she threw up.

Nancy knocked very gently. 'Mrs Warwick? Kate? Are you all right?'

She opened the door and leaned weakly against the frame. 'I ate some of those prawns that were left in the fridge last night. Perhaps you'd better throw them out.'

The girl looked at her a little oddly but nodded. 'Just you get back to bed. I'll call the doctor.'

'No.' She made an effort to stand upright. 'I'm fine now. I'll be all right.'

But she wasn't. The doctor ordered her to spend the rest of the day in bed and take it easy for the rest of the week.

'There's nothing wrong with you. You're just tired. It's quite normal in early pregnancy. Nancy will look after you; she's done it for her mother often enough.' He turned as the door opened. 'Jay, good to see you, dear boy. Now I've just been telling your wife to take things easy. No more of these late nights at discos for a while, do you hear?'

Jay stood in the doorway. 'I believe it was gadding about Suffolk that tired her.'

'Hmph! Well, make sure she gets plenty of rest, she's only a little thing after all.'

Jay followed the doctor from the room, returning a while later with a tray. 'I haven't had any lunch so I thought I'd have some with you. Nancy's chicken soup.'

'I'm sorry, Jay.'

He glanced up. 'Sorry?' A pulse was beating fiercely at his temple. 'Why are you sorry?'

'About the baby. I should have taken

precautions. I just didn't think . . . '

'On the whole, I think I prefer you when you're not thinking. Did I ask you to take precautions?'

'No, but . . . '

'In that case allow me to take responsibility for my own actions.' He stared at her. 'Unless, of course, you don't want my child?'

'Not want . . . ?' Words failed her. She flung back the covers and struggled to her feet. 'Damn you, Jay Warwick. Damn you. This is my child too! How dare you suggest I don't want him?' He caught her before she had taken a step and held her sobbing in his arms. 'I've messed up your life, Jay. How could I have been so stupid?' He picked her up and laid her back on the bed. 'This doesn't change anything. I'm going in September.'

'Him?' He laid his hand upon her stomach. 'You're so certain it's a boy? It's odd, but I was sure of a girl with black hair and grey eyes, just like her mother.'

'You knew?' She sighed. 'I tried to be so quiet when I was sick.'

'I knew before then, Kate.'

'But you couldn't. I didn't know myself . . . '

He pushed aside the creamy silk of her nightgown and cradled her breasts in his hands. They were fuller, lightly veined, different. No longer the breasts of an untried girl, but those of a woman. 'They are quite beautiful.' He bent and kissed each firm peak before covering her once more and pulling the sheet over her.

It was hard. But she had to say it now. Straight away. 'I mean it, Jay. I planned to go before you found out about the baby. This makes no difference.'

'You won't believe you said that when she's crying in the middle of the night,' he warned her.

'He!' Jay laughed. God, but she loved him so much. 'You made Annabel a promise, Jay. You must keep it.'

'On the subject of Annabel, I think you should see this.' He produced a stiff white card from his pocket.

She took the card. 'What is this?'

'An invitation to her wedding.'

She felt the blood drain from her face. He was so matter-of-fact. Annabel had seen him married to her and this was her response.

'Jay, you must tell her!'

'Tell her what?' he murmured. He had stretched out alongside her and was busy kissing her fingers. His lips were already moving to her wrist and she had to stop him.

'No! You can't let this happen!'

He looked up. 'Let what happen?' As the tears flowed once more he was all concern. 'Whatever is the matter?'

'I can't let you do this. Go to her. Tell her that in a few months you'll be free . . .'

'I think Charlie Mountjoy would take a dim view of that. And while Annabel would doubtless find the whole story amusing, I can assure you she's not about to take me under her duvet.' He pulled a face. 'I never could see the attraction of three in a bed . . . ' He smiled lazily down at her. 'Well, not if one of the other two is a bloke.'

'Stop trying to make a joke of it! I'm being serious, for heaven's sake. You accused me of making a martyr of myself — well, I'm not about to let you do the same.'

'Let me assure you, my love, that I'm thoroughly enjoying the sacrifice.'

'Jay, this is hard enough.' She turned away from him while she regained control. 'Just let me go away. No one will even notice.' She turned back, a bright smile fixed to her lips. 'I've been to look at some places in Suffolk. You were right, you know, about a country restaurant.' She sniffed. 'I really loved Beccles . . . '

His harsh execration on that charming town made her gasp. 'You are my wife, Kate. You are carrying my child. Do you think I would have married you if I loved someone else? Dear God! If you think that, no wonder you can't wait to get away from me.'

'But you said. We agreed. It was to be just an affair. Until September.'

'But I have every intention of taking up my option to renew. Didn't you know that? Sweet, noble Kate, prepared to sacrifice all happiness on the altar of family duty and who would even now stand aside for a rival.' He drew her into the circle of his arms. 'You have no rival, my darling.'

A long time later he raised his head. 'I was going to ask you to marry me that night. I had the champagne all ready.' Kate remembered the bottle cooling on the sideboard. 'I couldn't sleep after you had gone. I lay hour after hour wondering what on earth I was going to do about you and then it was all so blazingly obvious. I wanted you forever. And I had the feeling you might prove resistant to the idea. I knew that I would have to convince you that I would take on a whole chorus of sisters if you came with them.' He rocked her gently in his arms. 'I took myself quite by surprise.'

'You're taking me that way, right now,' she whispered.

'That David really did a job on you, didn't he? It must have seemed so easy to hide behind Sam.' He cradled her softly in his arms. 'And like an idiot I fell for it. Until you went out with Mike. That gave me pause for thought. I was beginning to understand you a little and I knew you had some strong attachment to Sam, whoever he was. And I didn't believe for one moment you would go out with one man when you were in love with another. So I changed my tactics. Gave you some space. Tried being gallant. I had the feeling you were almost disappointed . . . '

'I didn't notice much thinking, Jay Warwick,' she retaliated. 'You took very precipitate action, as I recall.'

'Can you blame me? The thought of Mike Howard kissing you . . . Then Sam fell into the lake and — '

'I fell into your bed.'

'I came racing back across the Atlantic, convinced that you were a ripe plum, ready for the plucking.' He shook his head at her sharp intake of breath. 'Shocking, I know. I'm ashamed of myself. I didn't even stop over in London. I drove straight up here and there you were, tucked up warm and willing in my bed and me half dead from exhaustion — '

'Are you saying you threw me out because you were tired?'

A smile trembled on his lips. 'I promise you that I wasn't that tired, my love, but I do have certain standards of performance to maintain.' She gasped. Then pushed him away as he laughed out loud. He pulled her back into his arms and held her close. 'No. Oh, darling, no. But when you put your arms around my neck, all trembling innocence, and said, 'Love me, Jay,' I almost fell apart. I didn't think I could ever love anyone again. I knew then that I had to have you for ever. Because I do love you, Kate. With all my heart. Quite an admission from an old cynic like me. Can you believe it?'

She held her breath, for a moment unable to speak with happiness. Then she lifted her head to look at him, a little furrow creasing her brow. 'But you spent the night before the wedding with Annabel.'

'With Annabel's parents. I had to stay somewhere. It wouldn't have done for us to have shared the same breakfast-table on the morning of our wedding. Shockingly bad luck. And the Courtneys are old friends. She had come down for the wedding too.'

'She really does want to marry someone else?'

'I imagine so. She never did anything that she hadn't organised with military precision.'

Kate picked up the invitation. 'Charles Mountjoy? Wasn't there a divorce a few months ago?'

'Yes, but nothing messy. He and Annabel have been seeing one another for years. Very quietly. Whenever interest in Annabel's doings became uncomfortably public I was hauled in to squire her about a bit. Put the news hounds off the scent. I insisted she return the favour by doing her level best to make you jealous.'

'She did, Jay. Oh, she did.'

'She was less than pleased to have her convenient escort hijacked by you, I can tell you.'

She recalled the overheard conversation. Now he had explained, it all had a completely different meaning. 'Well, she can't have you back.' She paused. 'But you already told her that, didn't you?'

He gave a sharp exclamation. 'You overheard us?'

She nodded. 'I thought you had gone back to her, when I saw you this morning on the television.'

'That was work, Kate. I love you. There aren't any other words to describe the way I feel about you.' But before she could tell him that she felt the same way he had moved on. 'Now tell me all about this restaurant in Beccles.'

'What restaurant?' she asked. 'I've

never heard of Beccles.'

He laughed. 'That's a relief. I was beginning to worry how you were going to run it, run Fullerton Hall and have a baby as well. And you should know that Annabel has worked everyone up into a furore of excitement about doing a television series from this kitchen. She seems to think she will have you to convince me.' He seemed a little tense as he waited for her response.

'I hope you told them that it was impossible.' She reached out and touched his cheek. 'I want you, Jay Warwick, not a television career.'

He caught her face between his hands and kissed her. 'Will you stay, Kate?'

She lay back against the pillows and smiled very slowly. 'Why don't you ask me again in September?'

* * *

Kate opened the church door. The scent of chrysanthemums from the

314

floral display near the altar mingled with dust and old hymn books. The light filtering through the stained glass of the main window was subdued but she could see Jay standing before the altar just as he had on their wedding-day, not turning, although he must have heard her.

She walked up the aisle, the sound of her footsteps echoing around the high ceiling. She had been by herself that day too. Then the church had been full and expectant, bursting with music and Jay had been waiting near the altar, staring ahead in that fixed way, not turning until at last she had stood beside him.

'Jay?' Her voice sounded unnaturally loud. 'What are you doing? Nancy said you wanted to see me in here.'

He turned to her then, his face grave. 'It's the last day of September, Kate.'

'Jay — '

'I've been thinking about the day we came here to be married. All those people watching us make our vows. I wonder what they would have thought if they had known that I had bullied you into marriage and that you would have done anything to have been a thousand miles away from me that day.'

'It wasn't like that.'

'Wasn't it? I knew that I loved you, I was sure you loved me, but it wasn't quite what it should have been, was it?'

She lowered her eyes. 'I'm sorry, Jay. I spoilt everything.'

'No. If there's blame to be apportioned I have no doubt the scales would be weighted rather more heavily on my side than on yours. I behaved very badly to you. Made assumptions about your character I had no right to make, except that even as I saw you in Harry Roberts' arms I felt something very like jealousy. Quite a shock to my system. And you took your revenge, so subtly that I might never have known but for Sam's accident. I underestimated you. Something, believe me, Kate, that I shall never do again.' He cleared his throat. 'I've been sitting here for hours, wondering what I would do if you decided after all that you didn't want to stay.'

'I — ' He stopped her, covering her mouth with his fingers.

'Let me finish.' He turned to face her, taking both her hands in his. 'Kate Warwick, before God, in this place, I want you to know that I love you with all my heart. I promise to love you and honour you all my days. Now I am asking you, will you stay with me as my wife? Be the mother of my children?'

The church, the coloured light from the stained glass windows, the flowers, all ran and blended into a ripple of colour as her eyes filled with tears. He had once demanded tears of happiness. Now, at last, they spilled down her cheeks. She blinked and looked up at him.

'Jay Warwick, before God, in this place, I want you to know that my heart, my soul, my life are yours. For as long as you want me.'

For a moment they both stood a little breathless and bemused. Then he leaned forward and touched her lips with his. 'Forever, my love. Until death us do part.'

THE END

Other titles in the
Linford Romance Library:

SONG OF MY HEART

Margaret Mounsdon

Andi Cox lands her dream job, looking after the two daughters of pop music icon Jas Summers. But when Jas starts arranging a summer charity concert in the grounds of his country house and the girls become the subject of kidnap threats, her troubles really begin . . . Along the way Andi acquires a new stepmother in the eccentric Hermione — and then she loses her heart to Jas . . .

TANGO AT MIDNIGHT

Cara Cooper

Nicci Tate has to play the part of entrepreneur to persuade bank manager Grant Blake to agree a loan. This would make her dream of opening her own shop come true. However, Nicci has demons in her past which could jeopardise everything — including Grant's growing fondness for her — and she cannot let him get too close. But Grant, who has a problem with theft at the bank and his own dark mystery, isn't a man who's easily turned away.

FLIGHTS OF FANCY

Sheila Holroyd

Jessica always does the sensible thing — until she meets James Strang . . . In Prague with friends, Jessica is grateful when a bag thief is foiled by James' intervention. Back home, although James lives in Birmingham and Jessica in Manchester, she finds herself agreeing to help James in his hour of need, and turning to him in hers. So when he suddenly vanishes from her life, Jessica is hurt and bewildered. Should she have just played it safe after all?